CHRISTMAS LETTERS

CHRISTMAS LETTERS

DEBBIE MACOMBER

WHEELER
CHIVERS

This Large Print edition is published by Wheeler Publishing, Waterville, Maine, USA and by BBC Audiobooks Ltd, Bath, England.
Wheeler Publishing is an imprint of The Gale Group.
Wheeler is a trademark and used herein under license.

LIBRARY OF CONGRESS CATALOGING-IN-PUBLICATION DATA

Macomber, Debbie.
  Christmas letters / by Debbie Macomber. — Large print ed.
    p. cm. — (Wheeler Publishing large print hardcover)
  ISBN-13: 978-1-59722-468-0 (hardcover : alk. paper)
  ISBN-10: 1-59722-468-5 (hardcover : alk. paper)
  1. Women — Washington (State) — Fiction. 2. Seattle (Wash.) — Fiction.
3. Christmas stories. 4. Large type books. I. Title.
PS3563.A2364C48 2007
813'.54—dc22   2007008983

BRITISH LIBRARY CATALOGUING-IN-PUBLICATION DATA AVAILABLE

Published in 2007 in the U.S. by arrangement with Harlequin Books S.A.
Published in 2007 in the U.K. by arrangement with Harlequin Enterprises II B.V.

U.K. Hardcover: 978 1 405 64244 6 (Chivers Large Print)
U.K. Softcover: 978 1 405 64245 3 (Camden Large Print)

Printed in the United States of America on permanent paper
10 9 8 7 6 5 4 3 2 1

C450726531

To Katherine Orr
Better known as K.O.
for her encouragement and support
through the years

PROLOGUE

Zelda O'Connor Davidson
76 Orchard Avenue
Seattle, Washington
Christmas, 2006

Dear Family and Friends:

Merry Christmas, everyone!

Let me warn you — this Christmas letter won't be as clever as last year's. My sister, Katherine (whom you may know better as K.O.), wrote that one for me but, ironically, she hasn't got time to do this year's. Ironic because it's due to the popularity of that particular letter that she's managed to start a little business on the side — writing Christmas letters for other people! (She offered to write mine, of course, but I know that between her work doing medical transcriptions, her job search and her Christmas letters, it would be a real stretch to find the time.)

So, here goes. The twins, Zoe and Zara, have recently turned five. They're looking forward to starting kindergarten next September. It's hard to believe our little girls are almost old enough for school! Still, they keep themselves (and us!) busy. So do our assorted pets — especially the dogs, two Yorkies named Zero and Zorro.

I'm still a stay-at-home mom and Zach's still working as a software programmer. This year's big news, which I want to share with all of you, has to do with a wonderful book I read. It changed my family's life. It's called *The Free Child* and it's by Dr. Wynn Jeffries. My sister scoffs at this, but Dr. Jeffries believes that children can be trusted to set their own boundaries. He also believes that, as parents, we shouldn't impose fantasies on them — fantasies like Santa Claus. Kids are capable of accepting reality, he says, and I agree! (See page 146 of *The Free Child*.)

So, this Christmas will be a different kind of experience for us, one that focuses on family, not fantasy.

Zach and the girls join me in wishing all of you a wonderful Christmas. And remember, a free child is a happy child (see page 16).

Love and kisses,

Zelda, Zach, Zoe and Zara

(and a wag of the tail from Zero & Zorro)

CHAPTER 1

It *was* him. Katherine O'Connor, better known as K.O., was almost positive. She squinted just to be sure. He looked identical to the man on the dust jacket of that ridiculous book, the one her sister treated like a child-rearing bible. Of course, people didn't really look like their publicity photos. And she hadn't realized the high and mighty Dr. Wynn Jeffries was from the Seattle area. Furthermore, she couldn't imagine what he was doing on Blossom Street.

She'd never even met him, but she distrusted him profoundly and disliked him just as much. It was because of Dr. Jeffries that she'd been banned from a local bookstore. She'd had a small difference of opinion with the manager on the subject of Wynn's book. Apparently the bookseller was a personal friend of his, because she'd leaped to Dr. Jeffries' defense and had ordered K.O. out of the store. She'd even suggested K.O. take her future book-purchasing business elsewhere, which seemed unnecessarily extreme.

"K.O.," Bill Mulcahy muttered, distracting her. They sat across from each other at the French Café, filled to capacity during the midmorning rush. People lined up for coffee, and another line formed at the bakery counter. "Did you get all that?" he asked.

"Sure," K.O. said, returning her attention to him. "Sorry — I thought I saw someone I knew." Oh, the things she was willing to do for some extra holiday cash. One witty Christmas letter written on her sister's behalf, and all of a sudden K.O. was the most sought-after woman at her brother-in-law's office. They all wanted her to write their Christmas letters. She'd been shocked to discover how much they'd willingly plunk down for it, too. Bill Mulcahy was the third person she'd met with this week, and his letter was the most difficult so far. Leno or Letterman would've had a hard time finding anything amusing about this man's life.

"I don't know what you're going to write," Bill continued. "It's been an exceptionally bad year. As I explained earlier, my son is in a detention home, my daughter's living with her no-good boyfriend and over Thanksgiving she announced she's pregnant. Naturally, marriage is out of the question."

"That *is* a bit of a challenge," K.O. agreed. She widened her eyes and stared again at the man who waited in the long line at the cash register. It *was* him; she was convinced of it now. The not-so-good doctor was — to put it in appropriately seasonal terms — a fruitcake. He was a child psychologist who'd written a book called *The Free Child* that was the current child-rearing rage.

To be fair, K.O. was single and not a mother. The only child-rearing experience she'd had was with her identical twin nieces, Zoe and Zara, whom she adored. Until recently, anyway. Overnight the five-year-olds had become miniature monsters and all because her sister had followed the "Free Child" rules as set out by Dr. Jeffries.

"My wife," Bill said, "is on the verge of a breakdown."

K.O. pitied the poor woman — and her husband.

"We've written Christmas letters for years and while life wasn't always as perfect as we — well, as we implied . . ." He let the rest fade away.

"You painted the picture of a model family."

"Yes." Bill cleared his throat and offered

her a weak smile. "Patti, that's my wife, chose to present a, shall we say, rosier depiction of reality." He exhaled in a rush. "We never included family pictures and if you met my son, you'd know why. Anyone looking at Mason would know in a minute that this kid isn't a member of the National Honor Society." He released his breath again and shook his head sadly. "Mason's into body piercing," Bill added. "He pierced his eyebrows, his nose, his lips, his tongue, his nipples —"

K.O. stopped him before he went any lower. "I get it."

"You probably don't, but that's lucky for you. Oh, and he dyed his hair green."

"Green?"

"He wears it spiked, too, and he . . . he does this thing with paint." Bill dropped his voice.

K.O. was sure she'd misunderstood. "I beg your pardon?"

"Mason doesn't call it paint. It's some form of cosmetic he smears across his face. I never imagined that my son would be rummaging through his mother's makeup drawer one day."

"I suppose that is a bit disconcerting," K.O. murmured.

"I forget the actual significance of the

14

black smudges under his eyes and across his cheeks," Bill said. "To me it looks like he's some teenage commando."

Yes, this letter would indeed be a challenge. "Have you thought about skipping your Christmas letter this year?" K.O. asked hopefully.

"Yeah, I'd like to, but as I said, Patti's emotional health is rather fragile. She claims people are already asking about our annual letter. She's afraid that if we don't send it the same as we do every year, everyone will figure out that we're pitiful parents." His shoulders drooped. "In other words, we've failed our children."

"I don't think you've necessarily *failed*," K.O. assured him. "Most teenagers go through a rebellious stage."

"Did you?"

"Oh, sure."

"Did you pierce anything?"

"Well, I had my ears pierced. . . ."

"That's not the same thing." He peered at her earrings, visible through her straight blond hair, which she wore loosely tied back. "And you only have one in each ear — not eight or ten like my son." He seemed satisfied that he'd proved his point. "Then you'll write our Christmas letter and smooth over the rough edges of our year?"

K.O. was less and less confident that she could pull this off. "I don't know if I'm your person," she said hesitantly. How could she possibly come up with a positive version of such a disastrous year? Besides, this side job was supposed to be fun, not real work. It'd begun as a favor to her sister and all of a sudden she was launching a career. At some stage she'd need to call a halt — maybe sooner than she'd expected.

Her client shifted in his seat. "I'll pay you double what you normally charge."

K.O. sat up straight. Double. He said he'd pay double? "Would four days be enough time?" she asked. Okay, so she could be bought. She pulled out her Day-Timer, checked her schedule and they set a date for their next meeting.

"I'll give you half now and half when you're finished."

That seemed fair. Not one to be overly prideful, she held out her hand as he peeled off three fifty-dollar bills. Her fingers closed around the cash.

"I'll see you Friday then," Bill said, and reaching for his briefcase, he left the French Café carrying his latte in its takeout cup.

Looking out the windows with their Christmas garland, she saw that it had begun to snow again. This was the coldest

December on record. Seattle's normally mild climate had dipped to below-freezing temperatures for ten days in a row. So much for global warming. There was precious little evidence of it in Seattle.

K.O. glanced at the coffee line. Wynn Jeffries had made his way to the front and picked up his hot drink. After adding cream and sugar — lots of both, she observed — he was getting ready to leave. K.O. didn't want to be obvious about watching him, so she took a couple of extra minutes to collect her things, then followed him out the door.

Even if she introduced herself, she had no idea what to say. Mostly she wanted to tell him his so-called Free Child movement — no boundaries for kids — was outright lunacy. How could he, in good conscience, mislead parents in this ridiculous fashion? Not that she had strong feelings on the subject or anything. Okay, so maybe she'd gone a little overboard at the bookstore that day, but she couldn't help it. The manager had been touting the benefits of Dr. Jeffries' book to yet another unsuspecting mom. K.O. felt it was her duty to let the poor woman know what might happen if she actually followed Dr. Jeffries' advice. The bookseller had strenuously disagreed and from then on, the situation had gotten out of hand.

Not wanting him to think she was stalking him, which she supposed she was, K.O. maintained a careful distance. If his office was in Seattle, it might even be in this neighborhood. After the renovations on Blossom Street a few years ago, a couple of buildings had been converted to office space. If she could discreetly discover where he practiced, she might go and talk to him sometime. She hadn't read his book but had leafed through it, and she knew he was a practicing child psychologist. She wanted to argue about his beliefs and his precepts, tell him about the appalling difference in her nieces' behavior since the day Zelda had adopted his advice.

She'd rather he didn't see her, so she dashed inconspicuously across the street to A Good Yarn, and darted into the doorway, where she pretended to be interested in a large Christmas stocking that hung in the display window. From the reflection in the window, she saw Dr. Jeffries walking briskly down the opposite sidewalk.

As soon as it was safe, she dashed from the yarn store to Susannah's Garden, the flower shop next door, and nearly fell over a huge potted poinsettia, all the while keeping her eyes on Dr. Jeffries. He proved one thing, she mused. Appearances were deceiving. He looked so . . . so normal. Who would've guessed that beneath that distinguished, sophisticated and — yes — handsome exterior lay such a fiend? Perhaps *fiend* was too strong a word. Yet she considered Wynn Jeffries' thinking to be nothing short of diabolical, if Zoe and Zara were anything to judge by.

No way!

K.O. stopped dead in her tracks. She watched as Wynn Jeffries paused outside her condo building, her very own building, entered the code and strolled inside.

Without checking for traffic, K.O. crossed the street again. A horn honked and brakes squealed, but she barely noticed. She was dumbfounded.

Speechless.

There had to be some mistake. Perhaps he was making a house call. No, that wasn't right. What doctor made house calls in this day and age? What psychologist made house calls *ever*? Besides, he didn't exactly look like the compassionate type. K.O. bit her lip and wondered when she'd become so cynical. It'd happened around the same time her sister read Dr. Jeffries' book, she decided.

The door had already closed before she got there. She entered her code and stepped inside just in time to see the elevator glide shut. Standing back, she watched the floor numbers flicker one after another.

"Katherine?"

K.O. whirled around to discover LaVonne Young, her neighbor and friend. LaVonne was the only person who called her Katherine. "What are you doing, dear?"

K.O. pointed an accusing finger past the elegantly decorated lobby tree to the elevator.

LaVonne stood in her doorway with her huge tomcat, named predictably enough, Tom, tucked under her arm. She wore a long shapeless dress that was typical of her wardrobe, and her long graying hair was drawn back in a bun. When K.O. had first met her, LaVonne had reminded her of the character Auntie Mame. She still did. "Something wrong with the elevator?" LaVonne asked.

"No, I just saw a man . . ." K.O. glanced back and noticed that the elevator had gone all the way up to the penthouse suite. That shouldn't really come as a shock. His book sales being what they were, he could easily afford the penthouse.

LaVonne's gaze followed hers. "That must

be Dr. Jeffries."

"You know him?" K.O. didn't bother to hide her interest. The more she learned, the better her chances of engaging him in conversation.

"Of course I know Dr. Jeffries," the retired accountant said. "I know everyone in the building."

"How long has he lived here?" K.O. demanded. She'd been in this building since the first week it was approved for occupation. So she should've run into him before now.

"I believe he moved in soon after the place was renovated. In fact, the two of you moved in practically on the same day."

That was interesting. Of course, there was a world of difference between a penthouse suite and the first-floor, one-bedroom unit she owned. Or rather, that the bank owned and she made payments on. With the inheritance she'd received from her maternal grandparents, K.O. had put a down payment on the smallest, cheapest unit available. It was all she could afford at the time — and all she could afford now. She considered herself lucky to get in when she did.

"His name is on the mailbox," LaVonne said, gesturing across the lobby floor to the mailboxes.

"As my sister would tell you, I'm a detail person." It was just the obvious she missed.

"He's a celebrity, you know," LaVonne whispered conspiratorially. "Especially since his book was published."

"Have you read it?" K.O. asked.

"Well, no, dear, I haven't, but then never having had children myself, I'm not too concerned with child-raising. However, I did hear Dr. Jeffries interviewed on the radio and he convinced me. His book is breaking all kinds of records. Apparently it's on all the bestseller lists. So there must be *something* to what he says. In fact, the man on the radio called Dr. Jeffries the new Dr. Spock."

"You've got to be kidding!" Jeffries' misguided gospel was spreading far and wide.

LaVonne stared at her. "In case you're interested, he's not married."

"That doesn't surprise me," K.O. muttered. Only a man without a wife and children could possibly come up with such ludicrous ideas. He didn't have a family of his own to test his theories on; instead he foisted them on unsuspecting parents like her sister, Zelda, and brother-in-law, Zach. The deterioration in the girls' behavior was dramatic, but Zelda insisted this was normal as they adjusted to a new regimen. They'd "find their equilibrium," she'd said, quoting the book. Zach, who worked long hours, didn't really seem to notice. The twins' misbehavior would have to be even more extreme to register on him.

"Would you like me to introduce you?" LaVonne asked.

"No," K.O. responded immediately. Absolutely not. Well, maybe, but not now. And not for the reasons LaVonne thought.

"Do you have time for tea?" LaVonne asked. "I wanted to tell you about the most recent class I attended. Fascinating stuff, just fascinating." Since her retirement, LaVonne had been at loose ends and signed up for a variety of workshops and evening classes.

"I learned how to unleash my psychic abilities."

"You're psychic?" K.O. asked.

"Yes, only I didn't know it until I took this class. I've learned so much," she said in wonder. "So much. All these years, my innate talent has lain there, unused and unfulfilled. It took this class to break it free and show me what I should've known all along. *I can see into the future.*" She spoke in a portentous whisper.

"You learned this after one class?"

"Madame Ozma claims I have been

blessed with the sight. She warned me not to waste my talents any longer."

This *did* sound fascinating. Well . . . bizarre, anyway. K.O. would have loved to hear all about the class, but she really needed to start work. In addition to writing Christmas letters — which she did only in November and December — she was a medical transcriptionist by training. It paid the bills and had allowed her to put herself through college to obtain a public relations degree. Now she was searching for a job in PR, which wasn't all that easy to find, even with her degree. She was picky, too. She wanted a job with a salary that would actually meet her expenses. Over the years she'd grown accustomed to a few luxuries, like regular meals and flush toilets.

Currently her résumé was floating around town. Anytime now, she was bound to be offered the perfect job. And in the meanwhile, these Christmas letters gave her some useful practice in creating a positive spin on some unpromising situations — like poor Bill Mulcahy's.

"I'd love a cup of tea, but unfortunately I've got to get to work."

"Perhaps tomorrow," LaVonne suggested.

"That would be great."

"I'll call upon my psychic powers and look

24

into your future if you'd like." She sounded completely serious.

"Sure," K.O. returned casually. Perhaps LaVonne could let her know when she'd find a job.

LaVonne's eyes brightened. "I'll study my class notes and then I'll tell you what I *see* for you."

"Thanks." She reached over and scratched Tom's ears. The big cat purred with pleasure.

With a bounce in her step, LaVonne went into her condo, closing the door with a slam that shook her Christmas wreath, decorated with golden moons and silver stars. K.O. headed for her own undecorated door, which was across the hall. Much as she disapproved of her sister's hero, she could hardly wait to tell Zelda the news.

CHAPTER 2

K.O. waited until she'd worked two hours straight before she phoned her sister. Zelda was a stay-at-home mom with Zoe and Zara, who were identical twins. Earlier in the year Zelda and Zach had purchased the girls each a dog. Two Yorkshire terriers, which the two girls had promptly named Zero and Zorro. K.O. called her sister's home the Land of Z. Even now, she wasn't sure how Zelda kept the girls straight, let alone the dogs. Even their barks sounded identical. *Yap. Yap* and *yap* with an occasional *yip* thrown in for variety, as if they sometimes grew bored with the sound of their own yapping.

Zelda answered on the third ring, sounding frazzled and breathless. "Yes?" she snapped into the phone.

"Is this a bad time?" K.O. asked.

"Oh, hi." The lack of enthusiasm was apparent. In addition to everything else, Dr.

Jeffries' theories had placed a strain on K.O.'s relations with her younger sister.

"Merry Christmas to you, too," K.O. said cheerfully. "Can you talk?"

"Sure."

"The girls are napping?"

"No," Zelda muttered. "They decided they no longer need naps. Dr. Jeffries says on page 125 of his book that children should be allowed to sleep when, and only when, they decide they're tired. Forcing them into regimented nap- and bedtimes, is in opposition to their biological natures."

"I see." K.O. restrained the urge to argue. "Speaking of Dr. Jeffries . . ."

"I know you don't agree with his philosophy, but this is the way Zach and I have chosen to raise our daughters. When you have a family of your own, you can choose how best to parent your children."

"True, but . . ."

"Sorry," Zelda cried. It sounded as if she'd dropped the phone.

In the background, K.O. could hear her sister shouting at the girls and the dogs. Her shouts were punctuated with the dogs' yapping. A good five minutes passed before Zelda was back.

"What happened?" K.O. asked, genuinely concerned.

"Oh, nothing."

"As I started to say, I saw Dr. Jeffries."

"On television?" Zelda asked, only half-interested.

"No, in person."

"Where?" All at once she had Zelda's attention.

"On Blossom Street. You aren't going to believe this, but he actually lives in my building."

"Dr. Jeffries? Get out of here!"

Zelda was definitely interested now. "Wait — I heard he moved to Seattle just before his book was published." She took a deep breath. "Wow! You really *saw* him?"

"Uh-huh."

"Oh, my goodness, did you talk to him? Is he as handsome in person as he is in his photo?"

Feeling about him the way she did, K.O. had to consider the question for a moment. "He's fairly easy on the eyes." That was an understatement but looks weren't everything. To her mind, he seemed stiff and unapproachable. Distant, even.

"Did you tell him that Zach and I both read his book and what a difference it's made in our lives?"

"No, but . . ."

"K.O., could you . . . Would it be too

28

much to get his autograph? Could you bring it on the fifteenth?"

K.O. had agreed to spend the night with the twins while Zelda and Zach attended his company's Christmas party. Her sister and brother-in-law had made arrangements to stay at a hotel downtown, just the two of them.

"All the mothers at the preschool would *die* to have Dr. Jeffries' autograph."

"I haven't met him," K.O. protested. It wasn't like she had any desire to form a fan club for him, either.

"But you just said he lives in your building."

"Yes."

"Are you sure it's him?"

"It looks like him. Anyway, LaVonne said it was."

Zelda gave a small shout of excitement. "If LaVonne says it's him, then it must be. How could you live in the same building as Dr. Jeffries and not know it?" her sister cried as though K.O. had somehow avoided this critical knowledge on purpose. "This is truly amazing. I've *got* to have his autograph."

"I'll . . . see what I can do," K.O. promised. This was not good. She'd hoped to find common ground with her sister, not become a . . . a go-between so Zelda could get her hero's autograph. Some hero! K.O.'s views on just about everything having to do with parenting were diametrically opposed to those purveyed by Dr. Wynn Jeffries. She'd feel like a fraud if she asked for his autograph.

"One more thing," Zelda said when her excitement had died down. "I know we don't agree on child-rearing techniques."

"That's true, but I understand these are your daughters." She took a deep breath. "How you raise them isn't really any of my business."

"Exactly," Zelda said emphatically. "Therefore, Zach and I want you to know we've decided to downplay Christmas this year."

"Downplay Christmas," K.O. repeated, not sure what that meant.

"We aren't putting up a tree."

"No Christmas tree!" K.O. sputtered, doing a poor job of hiding her disapproval. She couldn't imagine celebrating the holiday without decorating a tree. Her poor nieces would be deprived of a very important tradition.

"I might allow a small potted one for the kitchen table." Zelda seemed a bit doubtful herself. She *should* be doubtful, since a Christmas tree had always been part of their

30

own family celebration. The fact that their parents had moved to Arizona was difficult enough. This year they'd decided to take a cruise in the South Pacific over Christmas and New Year's. While K.O. was happy to see her mother and father enjoying their retirement, she missed them enormously.

"Is this another of Dr. Jeffries' ideas?" K.O. had read enough of his book — and heard *more* than enough about his theories — to suspect it was. Still, she could hardly fathom that even Wynn Jeffries would go this far. Outlaw Christmas? The man was a menace!

"Dr. Jeffries believes that misleading children about Santa does them lasting psychological damage."

"The girls can't have Santa, either?" This was cruel and unusual punishment. "Next you'll be telling me that you're doing away with the tooth fairy, too."

"Why, yes, of course. It's the same principle."

K.O. knew better than to argue with her sister. "Getting back to Christmas . . ." she began.

"Yes, Christmas. Like I said, Zach and I are planning to make it a low-key affair this year. Anything that involves Santa is out of the question."

Thankfully her sister was unable to see K.O. roll her eyes.

"In fact, Dr. Jeffries has a chapter on the subject. It's called 'Bury Santa Under the Sleigh.' Chapter eight."

"He wants to bury Santa Claus?" K.O. had heard enough. She'd personally bury Dr. Jeffries under a pile of plowed snow before she'd let him take Christmas away from Zoe and Zara. As far as she was concerned, his entire philosophy was unacceptable, but this no-Santa nonsense was too much. Here was where she drew her line in the snow — a line Wynn Jeffries had overstepped.

"Haven't you been listening to *anything* I've said?" Zelda asked.

"Unfortunately, I have."

Her doorbell chimed. "I need to go," K.O. told her sister. She sighed. "I'll see what I can do about that autograph."

"Yes, please," Zelda said with unmistakable gratitude. "It would mean the world to me if you could get Dr. Jeffries' autograph."

Sighing again, K.O. replaced the receiver and opened the door to find her neighbor LaVonne standing there. Although *standing* wasn't exactly the right word. LaVonne was practically leaping up and down. "I'm sorry to bother you but I just couldn't wait."

32

"Come in," K.O. said.

"I can't stay but a minute," the retired CPA insisted as she stepped over the threshold, clutching Tom. "I did it!" she exclaimed. "I saw the future." She squealed with delight and did a small jig. "I saw the future of your love life, K.O. It happened when I went to change the kitty litter."

"The . . . kitty litter." That was fitting, since it was where her love life happened to be at the moment. In some kind of toilet, anyway.

"Tom had just finished his business," LaVonne continued, gazing lovingly at her cat, "and there it was, plain as day."

"His business?" K.O. asked.

"No, no, the future. You know how some people with the *gift* can read tea leaves? Well, it came to me in the kitty-litter box. I know it sounds crazy but it's true. It was right there in front of me," she said. "You're going to meet the man of your dreams."

"Really?" K.O. hated to sound so disappointed. "I don't suppose you happened to see anything in the kitty litter about me finding a job?"

LaVonne shook her head. "Sorry, no. Do you think I should go back and look again? It's all in the way it's arranged in the kitty litter," she confided. "Just like tea leaves."

33

"Probably not." K.O. didn't want to be responsible for her neighbor sifting through Tom's "business" any more than necessary.

"I'll concentrate on your job prospects next."

"Great." K.O. was far more interested in locating full-time employment than falling in love. At twenty-eight she wasn't in a rush, although it *was* admittedly time to start thinking about a serious relationship. Besides, working at home wasn't conducive to meeting men. Zelda seemed to think that as a medical transcriptionist K.O. would meet any number of eligible physicians. That, however, hadn't turned out to be the case. The only person in a white coat she'd encountered in the last six months had been her dentist, and he'd been more interested in looking at her x-rays than at her.

"Before I forget," LaVonne said, getting ready to leave. "I'd like you to come over tomorrow for cocktails and appetizers."

"Sure." It wasn't as if her social calendar was crowded. "Thanks."

"I'll see you at six." LaVonne let herself out.

"Concentrate on seeing a job for me," K.O. reminded her, sticking her head in the hallway. "The next time you empty the litter box, I mean."

LaVonne nodded. "I will," she said. As she left, she was mumbling to herself, something K.O. couldn't hear.

The following morning, K.O. set up her laptop on a window table in the French Café, determined to wait for Dr. Jeffries. Now she felt obliged to get his autograph, despite her disapproval of his methods. More importantly, she had to talk to him about Christmas. This clueless man was destroying Christmas for her nieces — and for hundreds of thousands of other kids.

She had no intention of knocking on his door. No, this had to seem unplanned. An accidental meeting. Her one hope was that Wynn Jeffries was hooked on his morning latte. Since this was Seattle, she felt fairly certain he was. Nearly everyone in the entire state of Washington seemed to be a coffee addict.

In an effort to use her time productively, K.O. started work on the Mulcahy Christmas letter, all the while reminding herself that he was paying her double. She had two ideas about how to approach the situation. The first was comical, telling the truth in an outlandish manner and letting the reader assume it was some sort of macabre humor.

Merry Christmas from the Mulcahys, K.O.

wrote. She bit her lip and pushed away a strand of long blond hair that had escaped from her ponytail. *Bill and I have had a challenging year. Mason sends greetings from the juvenile detention center where he's currently incarcerated. Julie is pregnant and we pray she doesn't marry the father. Bill, at least, is doing well, although he's worried about paying for the mental care facility where I'm receiving outpatient therapy.*

K.O. groaned. This *wasn't* humorous, macabre or otherwise. It was difficult to turn the Mulcahys' disastrous year into comedy, especially since the letter was purportedly coming from them.

She deleted the paragraph and tried her second approach.

Merry Christmas from the Mulcahys, and what an — interesting? unexpected? unusual? — *year it has been for our lovely family.* K.O. decided on *eventful. Bill and I are so proud of our children, especially now as they approach adulthood. Where have all the years gone?*

Mason had an opportunity he couldn't turn down and is currently away at school. Our son is maturing into a fine young man and is wisely accepting guidance from authority figures. Our sweet Julie is in her second year of college. She and her boyfriend have de-

cided to deepen their relationship. Who knows, there might be wedding bells — and perhaps even a baby — in our daughter's future.

So intent was she on putting a positive spin on the sad details of Bill Mulcahy's year that she nearly missed Wynn Jeffries. When she looked up, it was just in time to see Dr. Jeffries walk to the counter. K.O. leaped to her feet and nearly upset her peppermint mocha, an extravagance she couldn't really afford. She remained standing until he'd collected his drink and then straightening, hurried toward him.

"Dr. Jeffries?" she asked, beaming a winsome smile. She'd practiced this very smile in front of the mirror before job interviews. After her recent cleaning at the dentist's, K.O. hoped she didn't blind him with her flashing white teeth.

"Yes?"

"You are Dr. Jeffries, Dr. Wynn Jeffries?"

"I am." He seemed incredibly tall as he stood in front of her. She purposely blocked his way to the door.

K.O. thrust out her hand. "I'm Katherine O'Connor. We live in the same building."

He smiled and shook her hand, then glanced around her. He seemed eager to escape.

"I can't tell you what a surprise it was when LaVonne pointed out that the author of *The Free Child* lived in our building."

"You know LaVonne Young?"

"Well, yes, she's my neighbor. Yours, too," K.O. added. "Would you care to join me?" She gestured toward her table and the empty chairs. This time of day, it was rare to find a free table. She didn't volunteer the fact that she'd set up shop two hours earlier in the hope of bumping into him.

He checked his watch as if to say he really didn't have time to spare.

"I understand *The Free Child* has hit every bestseller list in the country." Flattery just might work.

Wynn hesitated. "Yes, I've been most fortunate."

True, but the parents and children of America had been most *un*fortunate in her view. She wasn't going to mention that, though. At least not yet. She pulled out her chair on the assumption that he wouldn't refuse her.

He joined her, with obvious reluctance. "I think I've seen you around," he said, and sipped his latte.

It astonished her that he knew who she was, while she'd been oblivious to his presence. "My sister is a very big fan of yours.

38

She was thrilled when she heard I might be able to get your autograph."

"She's very kind."

"Her life has certainly changed since she read your book," K.O. commented, reaching for her mocha.

He shrugged with an air of modesty. "I've heard that quite a few times."

"Changed for the *worse*," K.O. muttered.

He blinked. "I beg your pardon?"

She couldn't contain herself any longer. "You want to take Santa away from my nieces! *Santa Claus.* Where's your heart? Do you know there are children all over America being deprived of Christmas because of *you?*" Her voice grew loud with the strength of her convictions.

Wynn glanced nervously about the room.

K.O. hadn't realized how animated she'd become until she noticed that everyone in the entire café had stopped talking and was staring in their direction.

Wynn hurriedly stood and turned toward the door, probably attempting to flee before she could embarrass him further.

"You're no better than . . . than Jim Carrey," K.O. wailed. She meant to say the Grinch who stole Christmas but it was the actor's name that popped out. He'd played the character in a movie a few years ago.

"Jim Carrey?" He turned back to face her.

"Worse. You're a . . . a regular Charles Dickens." She meant Scrooge, darn it. But it didn't matter if, in the heat of her anger, she couldn't remember the names. She just wanted to embarrass him. "That man," she said, stabbing an accusatory finger at Wynn, "wants to bury Santa Claus under the sleigh."

Not bothering to look back, Wynn tore open the café door and rushed into the street. "Good riddance!" K.O. cried and sank down at the table, only to discover that everyone in the room was staring at her.

"He doesn't believe in Christmas," she explained and then calmly returned to the Mulcahys' letter.

CHAPTER 3

The confrontation with Wynn Jeffries didn't go well, K.O. admitted as she changed out of her jeans and sweater later that same afternoon. When LaVonne invited her over for appetizers and drinks, K.O. hadn't asked if this was a formal party or if it would be just the two of them. Unwilling to show up in casual attire if her neighbor intended a more formal event, K.O. chose tailored black slacks, a white silk blouse and a red velvet blazer with a Christmas tree pin she'd inherited from her grandmother. The blouse was her very best. Generally she wore her hair tied back, but this evening she kept it down, loosely sweeping up one side and securing it with a rhinestone barrette. A little lip gloss and mascara, and she was ready to go.

A few minutes after six, she crossed the hall and rang LaVonne's doorbell. As if she'd been standing there waiting, LaVonne opened her door instantly.

K.O. was relieved she'd taken the time to change. Her neighbor looked lovely in a long skirt and black jacket with any number of gold chains dangling around her neck and at least a dozen gold bangles on her wrists.

"Katherine!" she cried, sounding as though it'd been weeks since they'd last spoken. "Do come in and meet Dr. Wynn Jeffries." She stepped back and held open the door and, with a flourish, gestured her inside.

Wynn Jeffries stood in the center of the room. He held a cracker raised halfway to his mouth, his eyes darting to and fro. He seemed to be gauging how fast he could make his exit.

Oh, dear. K.O. felt guilty about the scene she'd caused that morning.

"I believe we've met," Wynn said stiffly. He set the cracker down on his napkin and eyed the door.

Darn the man. He looked positively gorgeous, just the way he did on the book's dust jacket. This was exceedingly unfair. She didn't *want* to like him and she certainly didn't want to be attracted to him, which, unfortunately she was. Not that it mattered. She wasn't interested and after their con-

42

frontation that morning, he wouldn't be, either.

"Dr. Jeffries," K.O. murmured uneasily as she walked into the room, hands clasped together.

He nodded in her direction, then slowly inched closer to the door.

Apparently oblivious to the tension between them, LaVonne glided to the sideboard, where she had wine and liquor bottles set on a silver platter. Sparkling wineglasses and crystal goblets awaited their decision. "What can I pour for you?" she asked.

"I wouldn't mind a glass of merlot, if you have it," K.O. said, all the while wondering how best to handle this awkward situation.

"I do." LaVonne turned to Wynn. "And you, Dr. Jeffries?"

He looked away from K.O. and moved to stand behind the sofa. "Whiskey on the rocks."

"Coming right up."

"Can I help?" K.O. asked, welcoming any distraction.

"No, no, you two are my guests." And then as if to clear up any misconception, she added, "My *only* guests."

"Oh," K.O. whispered. A sick feeling attacked the pit of her stomach. She didn't glance at Wynn but suspected he was no more pleased at the prospect than she was.

A moment later, LaVonne brought their drinks and indicated that they should both sit down.

K.O. accepted the wine and Wynn took his drink.

With her own goblet in hand, LaVonne claimed the overstuffed chair, which left the sofa vacant. Evidently Dr. Jeffries was not eager to sit; neither was K.O. Finally she chose one end of the davenport and Wynn sat as far from her as humanly possible. Each faced away from the other.

"Wynn, I see you tried the crab dip," LaVonne commented, referring to the appetizers on the coffee table in front of them.

"It's the best I've ever tasted," he said, reaching for another cracker.

"I'm glad you enjoyed it. The recipe came from Katherine."

He set the cracker down and brushed the crumbs from his fingers, apparently afraid he was about to be poisoned.

K.O. sipped her wine in an effort to relax. She had a feeling that even if she downed the entire bottle, it wasn't going to help.

"I imagine you're wondering why I invited you here this evening," LaVonne said. Phillip, her white Persian, strolled regally into the room, his tail raised, and with one powerful thrust of his hind legs, leaped into her lap. LaVonne ran her hand down the length of his body, stroking his long, white fur. "It happened again," she announced, slowly enunciating the words.

"What happened?" Wynn asked, then gulped his drink.

Dramatically, LaVonne closed her eyes. "The sight."

Obviously not understanding, Wynn glanced at K.O., his forehead wrinkled.

"LaVonne took a class this week on unleashing your psychic abilities," K.O. explained under her breath.

Wynn thanked her for the explanation with a weak smile.

LaVonne's shoulders rose. "I have been gifted with the sight," she said in hushed tones.

"Congratulations," Wynn offered tentatively.

"She can read cat litter," K.O. told him.

"That's not all," LaVonne said, raising one hand. "As I said, it happened again. This morning."

"Not with the litter box?" K.O. asked.

"No." A distant look came over LaVonne as she fixed her gaze on some point across the room.

Peering over her shoulder, K.O. tried to figure out what her neighbor was staring at. She couldn't tell — unless it was the small decorated Christmas tree.

"I was eating my Raisin Bran and then, all of a sudden, I knew." She turned slightly to meet K.O.'s eyes. "The bran flakes separated, and that was when two raisins bobbed to the surface."

"You saw . . . the future?" K.O. asked.

"What she saw," Wynn muttered, "was two raisins in the milk."

LaVonne raised her hand once more, silencing them. "I saw the *future*. It was written in the Raisin Bran even more clearly than it'd been in the cat litter." She pointed a finger at K.O. "Katherine, it involved *you*."

"Me." She swallowed, not sure whether to laugh or simply shake her head.

"And you." LaVonne's finger swerved toward Wynn. Her voice was low and intent.

"Did it tell you Katherine would do her utmost to make a fool of me at the French Café?" Wynn asked. He scooped up a handful of mixed nuts.

As far as K.O. was concerned, *nuts* was an appropriate response to her neighbor's fortune-telling.

LaVonne dropped her hand. "No." She turned to K.O. with a reproachful frown.

"Katherine, what did you do?"

"I . . ." Flustered she looked away. "Did . . . did you know Dr. Jeffries doesn't believe in Santa Claus?" There, it was in the open now.

"My dear girl," LaVonne said with a light laugh. "I hate to be the one to disillusion you, but there actually *isn't* a Santa."

"There is if you're five years old," she countered, glaring at the man on the other end of the sofa. "Dr. Jeffries is ruining Christmas for children everywhere." The man deserved to be publicly ridiculed. Reconsidering, she revised the thought. "He should be censured by his peers for even *suggesting* that Santa be buried under the sleigh."

"It appears you two have a minor difference of opinion," LaVonne said, understating the obvious.

"I sincerely doubt Katherine has read my entire book."

"I don't need to," she said. "My sister quotes you chapter and verse in nearly every conversation we have."

"This is the sister who asked for my autograph?"

"Yes," K.O. admitted. Like most men, she concluded, Dr. Jeffries wasn't immune to flattery.

"She's the one with the children?"

K.O. nodded.

"Do you have children?"

LaVonne answered for her. "Katherine is single, the same as you, Wynn."

"Why doesn't that surprise me?" he returned.

K.O. thought she might have detected a smirk in his reply. "It doesn't surprise me that you're single, either," she said, elevating her chin. "No woman in her right mind —"

"My dears," LaVonne murmured. "You're being silly."

K.O. didn't respond, and neither did Wynn. "Don't you want to hear what I saw in my cereal?"

Phillip purred contentedly as LaVonne continued to stroke his fluffy white fur.

"The future came to me and I saw —" she paused for effect "— I saw the two of you. Together."

"Arguing?" Wynn asked.

"No, no, you were in love. Deeply, deeply in love."

K.O. placed her hand over her heart and gasped, and then almost immediately that remark struck her as the most comical thing she'd ever heard. The fact that LaVonne was reading her future, first in cat litter and now

Raisin Bran, was ridiculous enough, but to match K.O. up with Wynn — It was too much. She broke into peals of laughter. Pressing her hand over her mouth, she made an effort to restrain her giggles.

Wynn looked at her curiously.

LaVonne frowned. "I'm serious, Katherine."

"I'm sorry. I don't mean to be rude. LaVonne, you're my friend and my neighbor, but I'm sorry, it'll never happen. Never in a million years."

Wynn straightened. "While Katherine and I clearly don't see eye to eye on any number of issues, I tend to agree with her on this."

LaVonne sighed expressively. "Our instructor, Madam Ozma, warned us this would happen," she said with an air of sadness. "Unbelievers."

"It isn't that I don't believe you," K.O. rushed to add. She didn't want to offend LaVonne, whose friendship she treasured, but at the same time she found it difficult to play along with this latest idea of hers. Still, the possibility of a romance with just about anyone else would have suited her nicely.

"Wynn?" LaVonne said. "May I ask how you feel about Katherine?"

"Well, I didn't officially meet her until this

morning."

"I might've given him the wrong impression," K.O. began. "But —"

"No," he said swiftly. "I think I got the right impression. You don't agree with me and I had the feeling that for some reason you don't like me."

"True . . . well, not exactly. I don't know you well enough to like or dislike you."

LaVonne clapped her hands. "Perfect! This is just perfect."

Both K.O. and Wynn turned to her. "You don't really know each other, isn't that correct?" she asked.

"Correct," Wynn replied. "I've seen Katherine around the building and on Blossom Street occasionally, but we've never spoken — until the unfortunate incident this morning."

K.O. felt a little flustered. "We didn't start off on the right foot." Then she said in a conciliatory voice, "I'm generally not as confrontational as I was earlier today. I might've gotten a bit . . . carried away. I apologize." She did feel guilty for having embarrassed him and, in the process, herself.

Wynn's dark eyebrows arched, as if to say he was pleasantly surprised by her admission of fault.

"We all, at one time or another, say things we later regret," LaVonne said, smiling down on Phillip. She raised her eyes to K.O. "Isn't that right, Katherine?"

"Yes, I suppose so."

"And some of us," she went on, looking at Wynn, "make hasty judgments."

He hesitated. "Yes. However in this case —"

"That's why," LaVonne said, interrupting him, "I took the liberty of making a dinner reservation for the two of you. Tonight — at seven-thirty. An hour from now."

"A dinner reservation," K.O. repeated. Much as she liked and respected her neighbor, there was a limit to what she was willing to do.

"It's out of the question," Wynn insisted.

"I appreciate what you're doing, but . . ." K.O. turned to Wynn for assistance.

"I do, as well," he chimed in. "It's a lovely gesture on your part. Unfortunately, I have other plans for this evening."

"So do I." All right, K.O.'s plans included eating in front of the television and watching *Jeopardy,* and while those activities might not be anything out of the ordinary, they did happen to be her plans.

"Oh, dear." LaVonne exhaled loudly. "Chef Jerome Ray will be so disappointed not to meet my friends."

If Wynn didn't recognize the name, K.O. certainly did. "You know Chef Jerome Ray?"

"Of Chez Jerome?" Wynn inserted.

"Oh, yes. I did his taxes for years and years. What most people don't realize is that Jerome is no flash in the pan, if you'll excuse the pun. In fact, it took him twenty years to become an overnight success."

The Seattle chef had his own cooking show on the Food Network, which had become an immediate hit. His techniques with fresh seafood had taken the country by storm. The last K.O. had heard, it took months to get a reservation at Chez Jerome.

"I talked to Jerome this afternoon and he said that as a personal favor to me, he would personally see to your dinner."

"Ah . . ." K.O. looked at Wynn and weighed her options.

"Dinner's already paid for," LaVonne said in an encouraging voice, "and it would be a shame to let it go to waste."

A nuked frozen entrée and *Jeopardy,* versus one dinner with a slightly contentious man in a restaurant that would make her the envy of her friends. "I might be able to rearrange my plans," K.O. said after clearing her throat. Normally she was a woman of conviction. But in these circumstances, for a fabulous free dinner, she was willing to compromise.

"I think I can do the same," Wynn muttered.

LaVonne smiled brightly and clapped her hands. "Excellent. I was hoping you'd say that."

"With certain stipulations," Wynn added.

"Yes," K.O. said. "There would need to be stipulations."

Wynn scowled at her. "We will *not* discuss my book or my child-rearing philosophies."

"All right," she agreed. That sounded fair. "And we'll . . . we'll —" She couldn't think of any restriction of her own, so she said, "We refuse to overeat." At Wynn's frown, she explained, "I'm sort of watching my weight."

He nodded as though he understood, which she was sure he didn't. What man really did?

"All I care about is that the two of you have a marvelous dinner, but I know you will." LaVonne smiled at them both. "The raisins have already assured me of that." She studied her watch, gently dislodged Phillip and stood. "You'll need to leave right away. The reservation's under my name," she said and ushered them out the door.

Before she could protest or comment,

K.O. found herself standing in the hallway with Wynn Jeffries, her dinner date.

CHAPTER 4

If nothing else, K.O. felt this dinner would afford her the opportunity to learn about Wynn. Well, that and an exceptional dining experience, of course. Something in his background must have prompted a child-rearing ideology that in her opinion was completely impractical and threatened to create a generation of spoiled, self-involved brats. Although she didn't have children of her own, K.O. had seen the effect on her nieces ever since Zelda had read that darn book. She was astonished by how far her sister had been willing to go in following the book's precepts, and wondered if Zach understood the full extent of Zelda's devotion to *The Free Child.* Her brother-in-law was quite the workaholic. He was absorbed in his job and often stayed late into the evenings and worked weekends.

Chez Jerome was only a few blocks from Blossom Street, so K.O. and Wynn decided to walk. She retrieved a full-length red wool coat from her condo while Wynn waited outside the building. The moment she joined him, she was hit by a blast of cold air. A shiver went through her, and she hunched her shoulders against the wind. To her surprise, Wynn changed places with her, walking by the curb, outside the shelter of the buildings, taking the brunt of the wind. It was an old-fashioned gentlemanly action and one she hadn't expected. To be fair, she didn't know *what* to expect from him. With that realization came another. He didn't know her, either.

They didn't utter a single word for the first block.

"Perhaps we should start over," she suggested.

Wynn stopped walking and regarded her suspiciously. "You want to go back? Did you forget something?"

"No, I meant you and me."

"How so?" He kept his hands buried in the pockets of his long overcoat.

"Hello," she began. "My name is Katherine O'Connor, but most people call me K.O. I don't believe we've met."

He frowned. "We did earlier," he said.

"This is pretend." Did the man have to be so literal? "I want you to erase this morning from your memory and pretend we're meeting for the first time."

"What about drinks at LaVonne's? Should I forget that, too?"

"Well." She needed to think this over. That hadn't been such a positive experience, either. "Perhaps it would be best," she told him.

"So you want me to act as if this is a blind date?" he asked.

"A blind date," she repeated and immediately shook her head. "I've had so many of those, I need a seeing eye dog."

He laughed, and the sound of it was rich and melodious. "Me, too."

"You?" A man this attractive and successful required assistance meeting women?

"You wouldn't believe how many friends have a compulsion to introduce me to *the woman of my dreams.*"

"My friends say the same thing. *This* is the man you've been waiting to meet your entire life. Ninety-nine percent of the time, it's a disaster."

"Really? Even you?" He seemed a little shocked that she'd had help from her matchmaking friends.

"What do you mean *even you?*"

"You're blond and beautiful — I thought you were joking about those blind dates."

She swallowed a gasp of surprise. However, if that was the way he saw her, she wasn't going to argue.

He thrust out his hand. "Hello, Katherine, my name is Jim Carrey."

She laughed and they shook hands. They continued walking at a leisurely pace, and soon they were having a lively conversation, exchanging dating horror stories. She laughed quite a few times, which was something she'd never dreamed she'd do with Wynn Jeffries.

"Would you mind if I called you Katherine?" he asked.

"Not at all. Do you prefer Wynn or Dr. Jeffries?"

"Wynn."

"I've heard absolutely marvelous things about Chez Jerome," she said. Not only that, some friends of K.O.'s had recently phoned to make dinner reservations and were told the first available opening was in May.

"LaVonne is certainly full of surprises," Wynn remarked. "Who would've guessed she had a connection with one of the most popular chefs in the country?"

They arrived at the restaurant, and Wynn held the door for her, another gentlemanly courtesy that made her smile. This psychologist wasn't what she'd expected at all. After hearing his theories about Christmas, she'd been sure he must be a real curmudgeon. But in the short walk from Blossom Street to the restaurant, he'd disproved almost every notion she'd had about him. Or at least about his personality. His beliefs were still a point of contention.

When Wynn mentioned LaVonne's name to the maître d', they were ushered to a secluded booth. "Welcome to Chez Jerome," the man said with a dignified bow.

K.O. opened her menu and had just started to read it when Jerome himself appeared at their table. "Ah, so you are LaVonne's friends."

K.O. didn't mean to gush, but this was a real honor. "I am so excited to meet you," she said. She could hardly wait to tell Zelda about this — even though her sister would be far more impressed by her meeting Wynn Jeffries than Jerome.

The chef, in his white hat and apron, kissed her hand. The entire restaurant seemed to be staring at them and whispering, wondering who they were to warrant a visit from the renowned chef.

"You won't need those," Jerome said and ostentatiously removed the tasseled menus from their hands. "I am preparing a meal for you personally. If you do not fall in love after what I have cooked, then there is no hope for either of you."

Wynn caught her eye and smiled. Despite herself, K.O. smiled back. After a bit of small talk, Jerome returned to the kitchen.

Once the chef had gone, Wynn leaned toward her and teased, "He makes it sound as if dinner is marinated in Love Potion Number Nine." To emphasize the point, he sang a few lines from the old song.

K.O. smothered a giggle. She hated to admit it, but rarely had she been in a more romantic setting, with the elegant linens, flattering candlelight and soft classical music. The mood was flawless; so was their dinner, all four courses, even though she couldn't identify the exact nature of everything they ate. The appetizer was some kind of soup, served in a martini glass, and it tasted a bit like melted sherbet. Later, when their waiter told them the soup featured sea urchin, K.O. considered herself fortunate not to have known. If she had, she might not have tasted it. But, in fact, it was delicious.

"Tell me about yourself," she said to Wynn when the soup dishes were taken away and the salads, which featured frilly greens and very tart berries, were delivered.

He shrugged, as though he didn't really have anything of interest to share. "What would you like to know?"

"How about your family?"

"All right." He leaned back against the luxurious velvet cushion. "I'm an only child. My mother died three years ago. My father is Max Jeffries." He paused, obviously waiting to see if she recognized the name and when she didn't, he continued. "He was a surfer who made a name for himself back in the late sixties and early seventies."

She shook her head. Surfing wasn't an activity she knew much about, but then she really wasn't into sports. Or exercise, either. "My dad's the captain of his bowling team," she told him.

He nodded. "My parents were hippies." He grinned. "True, bona fide, unreconstructed hippies."

"As in the Age of Aquarius, free love and that sort of thing?" This explained quite a bit, now that she thought about it. Wynn had apparently been raised without boundaries himself and had turned out to be a successful and even responsible adult. Maybe he figured that would be true of any child raised according to his methods.

Wynn nodded again. "Dad made it rich when he was awarded a patent for his surfboard wax. Ever heard of Max's Waxes?" He sipped his wine, a lovely mellow pinot gris. K.O. did, too, savoring every swallow.

"I chose my own name when I was ten," he murmured.

It was hardly necessary to say he'd lived an unconventional life. "Why did you decide on Wynn?" she asked, since it seemed an unusual first name.

"It was my mother's maiden name."

"I like it."

"Katherine is a beautiful name," he commented. "A beautiful name for a beautiful woman."

If he didn't stop looking at her like that, K.O. was convinced she'd melt. This romantic rush was more intense than anything she'd ever experienced. She wasn't even prepared to *like* Wynn, and already she could feel herself falling for this son of a hippie. In an effort to break his spell, she forced herself to look away.

"Where did you grow up?" she asked as their entrées were ceremoniously presented. Grilled scallops with wild rice and tiny Brussels sprouts with even tinier onions.

"California," he replied. "I attended Berkeley."

"I lived a rather conventional life," she said after swooning over her first bite.

"Regular family, one sister, two parents. I studied to become a medical transcriptionist, worked for a while and returned to college. I have a degree in public relations, but I'm currently working from home as a transcriptionist while looking for full-time employment. I'd really like to work as a publicist, but those jobs are rare and the pay isn't all that great." She closed her eyes. "Mmm. I think this is the best meal I've ever had." And she wasn't referring *just* to the food.

He smiled. "Me, too."

A few minutes later, he asked, "Your sister is married with children?"

"Identical twin girls. Zoe and Zara. I'm their godmother." When she discussed the twins, she became animated, telling him story after story. "They're delightful," she finally said. Dessert and coffee arrived then. An unusual cranberry crème brûlée, in honor of the season, and cups of exquisite coffee.

"So you like children?" Wynn asked when they'd made serious progress with their desserts.

"Oh, yes," she said, then added a qualifier, "especially well-behaved children."

His eyebrows arched.

Seeing how easy it was to get sidetracked,

she said, "I think children are a subject we should avoid."

"I agree." But Wynn's expression was good-natured, and she could tell he hadn't taken offense.

Even after a two-and-a-half-hour dinner, K.O. was reluctant to leave. She found Wynn truly fascinating. His stories about living in a commune, his surfing adventures — including an encounter with a shark off the coast of Australia — and his travels kept her enthralled. "This has been the most wonderful evening," she told him. Beneath the polished exterior was a remarkable human being. She found him engaging and unassuming and, shock of shocks, *likeable.*

After being assured by Jerome that their meal had already been taken care of, Wynn left a generous tip. After fervent thanks and a protracted farewell, they collected their coats. Wynn helped K.O. on with hers, then she wrapped her scarf around her neck.

When they ventured into the night, they saw that snow had begun to fall. The Seattle streets were decorated for the season with sparkling white lights on the bare trees. The scene was as festive as one could imagine. A horse-drawn carriage passed them, the horse's hooves clopping on the pavement, its harness jingling.

"Shall we?" Wynn asked.

K.O. noticed that the carriage was traveling in the opposite direction from theirs, but she couldn't have cared less. For as long as she could remember, she'd wanted a carriage ride. "That would be lovely." Not only was Wynn a gentleman, but a romantic, as well, which seemed quite incongruous with his free-and-easy upbringing.

Wynn hailed the driver. Then he handed K.O. into the carriage before joining her. He took the lap robe, spread it across her legs, and slipped his arm around her shoulders. It felt like the most natural thing in the world to be in his embrace.

"I love Christmas," K.O. confessed.

Wynn didn't respond, which was probably for the best, since he'd actually put in writing that he wanted to bury Santa Claus.

The driver flicked the reins and the carriage moved forward.

"It might surprise you to know that I happen to feel the same way you do about the holidays."

"But you said —"

He brought a finger to her lips. "We agreed not to discuss my book."

"Yes, but I *have* to know. . . ."

"Then I suggest you read *The Free Child.* You'll understand my philosophies better once you do. Simply put, I feel it's wrong to mislead children. That's all I really said. Can you honestly object to that?"

"If it involves Santa, I can."

"Then we'll have to agree to disagree."

She was happy to leave that subject behind. The evening was perfect, absolutely perfect, and she didn't want anything to ruin it. With large flakes of snow drifting down and the horse clopping steadily along, the carriage swaying, it couldn't have been more romantic.

Wynn tightened his arm around her and K.O. pressed her head against his shoulder.

"I'm beginning to think LaVonne knows her Raisin Bran," Wynn whispered.

She heard the smile in his voice. "And her cat litter," she whispered back.

"I like her cats," he said. "Tom, Phillip and . . ."

"Martin," she supplied. The men in her neighbor's life all happened to be badly spoiled and much-loved cats.

The carriage dropped them off near West Lake Center. Wynn got down first and then helped K.O. "Are you cold?" he asked. "I can try to find a cab if you'd prefer not to walk."

"Stop," she said suddenly. All this perfection was confusing, too shocking a contrast with her previous impressions of Dr. Wynn Jeffries.

He frowned.

"I don't know if I can deal with this." She started walking at a fast pace, her mind spinning. It was difficult to reconcile this thoughtful, interesting man with the hard-hearted destroyer of Christmas Zelda had told her about.

"Deal with *what?*" he asked, catching up with her.

"You — you're wonderful."

He laughed. "That's bad?"

"It's not what I expected from you."

His steps matched hers. "After this morning, I wasn't sure what to expect from you, either. There's a big difference between the way you acted then and how you've been this evening. *I* didn't change. You did."

"I know." She looked up at him, wishing she understood what was happening. She recognized attraction when she felt it, but could this be real?

He reached for her hand and tucked it in the crook of his arm. "Does it matter?" he asked.

"Not for tonight," she said with a sigh.

"Good." They resumed walking, more slowly this time. She stuck out her tongue to catch the falling snow, the way she had as a child. Wynn did, too, and they both smiled, delighted with themselves and each other.

When they approached their building on Blossom Street, K.O. was almost sad. She didn't want the evening to end for fear she'd wake in the morning and discover it had all been a dream. Worse, she was afraid she'd find out it was just an illusion created by candlelight and gorgeous food and an enchanting carriage ride.

She felt Wynn's reluctance as he keyed in the door code. The warmth that greeted them inside the small lobby was a welcome respite from the cold and the wind. The Christmas lights in the lobby twinkled merrily as he escorted her to her door.

"Thank you for one of the most romantic evenings of my life," she told him sincerely.

"I should be the one thanking you," he whispered. He held her gaze for a long moment. "May I see you again?"

She nodded. But she wasn't sure that was wise.

"When?"

K.O. leaned against her door and held her hand to her forehead. The spell was wearing off. *"I don't think this is a good idea."* That was what she'd *intended* to say. Instead, when she opened her mouth, the words that popped out were, "I'm pretty much free all week."

He reached inside his overcoat for a PDA. "Tomorrow?"

"Okay." How could she agree so quickly, so impulsively? Every rational thought told her this relationship wasn't going to work. At some point — probably sooner rather than later — she'd have to acknowledge that they had practically nothing in common.

"Six?" he suggested.

With her mind screaming at her to put an end to this *now*, K.O. pulled out her Day-Timer and checked her schedule. Ah, the perfect excuse. She already had a commitment. "Sorry, it looks like I'm booked. I have a friend who's part of the Figgy Pudding contest."

"I beg your pardon?"

"Figgy Pudding is a competition for singing groups. It's a fund-raising event," she explained, remembering that he was relatively new to the area. "I told Vickie I'd come and cheer her on." Then, before she could stop herself, she added, "Want to join me?"

Wynn nodded. "Sure. Why not."

"Great." But it wasn't great. During her most recent visit with Vickie, K.O. had ranted about Dr. Jeffries for at least ten minutes. And now she was going to be introducing her friend to the man she'd claimed was ruining America. Introducing him as her . . . *date?*

She had to get out of this.

Then Wynn leaned forward and pressed his mouth to hers. It was such a nice kiss, undemanding and sweet. Romantic, too, just as the entire evening had been. In that moment, she knew exactly what was happening and why, and it terrified her. She liked Wynn. Okay, *really* liked him. Despite his crackpot theories and their total lack of compatibility. And it wasn't simply that they'd spent a delightful evening together. A charmed evening. No, this had all the hallmarks of a dangerous infatuation. Or worse.

Wynn Jeffries! Who would've thought it?

CHAPTER 5

The phone woke K.O. out of a dead sleep. She rolled over, glanced at the clock on her nightstand and groaned. It was already past eight. Lying on her stomach, she reached for the phone and hoped it wasn't a potential employer, asking her to come in for an interview that morning. Actually, she prayed it *was* a job interview but one with more notice.

"Good morning," she said in her best businesslike voice.

"Katherine, it's LaVonne. I didn't phone too early, did I?"

In one easy motion, K.O. drew herself into a sitting position, swinging her legs off the bed. "Not at all." She rubbed her face with one hand and stifled a yawn.

"So," her neighbor breathed excitedly. "How'd it go?"

K.O. needed a moment to consider her response. LaVonne was obviously asking about her evening with Wynn; however, she hadn't had time to analyze it yet. "Dinner was incredible," she offered and hoped that would satisfy her friend's curiosity.

"Of course dinner was incredible. Jerome promised me it would be. I'm talking about you and Wynn. He's very nice, don't you think? Did you notice the way he couldn't take his eyes off you? Didn't I tell you? It's just as I saw in the kitty litter and the Raisin Bran. You two are *meant* for each other."

"Well," K.O. mumbled, not knowing which question to answer first. She'd prefer to avoid them all. She quickly reviewed the events of the evening and was forced to admit one thing. "Wynn wasn't anything like I expected."

"He said the same about you."

"You've talked to him?" If K.O. wasn't awake before, she certainly was now. "What did he say?" she asked in a rush, not caring that LaVonne would realize how interested she was.

"Exactly that," LaVonne said. "Wynn told me you were nothing like he expected. He didn't know what to think when you walked into my condo. He was afraid the evening would end with someone calling the police — and then he had a stupendous night. That was the word he used — *stupendous.*"

"Really." K.O. positively glowed with pleasure.

"He had the look when he said it, too."

"What look?"

"The *look*," LaVonne repeated, emphasizing the word, "of a man who's falling in love. You had a good time, didn't you?"

"I did." K.O. doubted she could have lied. She *did* have a wonderful evening. Shockingly wonderful, in fact, and that made everything ten times worse. She wanted to view Wynn as a lunatic confounding young parents, a grinch out to steal Christmas from youngsters all across America. How could she berate him and detest him if she was in danger of falling in love with him? This was getting worse and worse.

"I knew it!" LaVonne sounded downright gleeful. "From the moment I saw those raisins floating in the milk, I knew. The vision told me everything."

"Everything?"

"Everything," LaVonne echoed. "It came to me, as profound as anything I've seen with my psychic gift. You and Dr. Jeffries are perfect together."

K.O. buried her face in her hand. She'd fallen asleep in a haze of wonder and awakened to the shrill ring of her phone. She couldn't explain last night's feelings in any rational way.

She wasn't attracted to Wynn, she told herself. How could she be? The man who believed children should set their own rules? The man who wanted to eliminate Santa Claus? But she was beginning to understand what was going on here. For weeks she'd been stuck inside her condo, venturing outside only to meet Christmas-letter clients. If she wasn't transcribing medical records, she was filling out job applications. With such a lack of human contact, it was only natural that she'd be swept along on the tide of romance LaVonne had so expertly arranged for her.

"Wynn told me you were seeing him again this evening," LaVonne said eagerly.

"I am?" K.O. vaguely remembered that. "Oh, right, I am." Her mind cleared and her memory fell into place like an elevator suddenly dropping thirteen floors. "Yes, as it happens," she said, trying to think of a way out of this. "I invited Wynn to accompany me to the Figgy Pudding event at West Lake Plaza." She'd *invited* him. What was she thinking? *What was she thinking?* Mentally she slapped her hand against her forehead. Before this afternoon, she had to find an excuse to cancel.

"He's very sweet, isn't he?" LaVonne said.

"He is." K.O. didn't want to acknowledge it but he was. He'd done it on purpose; she just didn't know *why.* What was his purpose in breaking down her defenses?

She needed to think. She pulled her feet up onto the bed and wrapped one arm around her knees. He *had* been sweet and alarmingly wonderful. Oh, he was clever. But what was behind all that charm? Nothing good, she'd bet.

"I have more to tell you," LaVonne said, lowering her voice to a mere whisper. "It happened again this morning." She paused. "I was feeding the boys."

K.O. had half a mind to stop her friend, but for some perverse reason she didn't.

"And then," LaVonne added, her voice gaining volume, "when I poured the dry cat food into their bowls, some of it spilled on the floor."

"You got a reading from the cat food?" K.O. supposed this shouldn't surprise her. Since LaVonne had taken that class, everything imaginable provided her with insight — mostly, it seemed, into K.O.'s life. Her love life, which to this point had been a blank slate.

"Would you like to know how many children you and Wynn are going to have?" LaVonne asked triumphantly.

"Any twins?" K.O. asked, playing along. She might as well. LaVonne was determined to tell her, whether she wanted to hear or not.

"Twins," LaVonne repeated in dismay. "Oh, my goodness, I didn't look that closely."

"That's fine."

LaVonne took her seriously. "Still, twins are definitely a possibility. Sure as anything, I saw three children. Multiple births run in your family, don't they? Because it might've been triplets."

"Triplets?" It was too hard to think about this without her morning cup of coffee. "Listen, I need to get off the phone. I'll check in with you later," K.O. promised.

"Good. You'll give me regular updates, won't you?"

"On the triplets?"

"No," LaVonne returned, laughing. "On you and Wynn. The babies come later."

"Okay," she said, resigned to continuing the charade. Everything might've been delightful and romantic the night before, but this was a whole new day. She was beginning to figure out his agenda. She'd criticized his beliefs, especially about Christmas, and now he was determined to change hers. It was all a matter of pride. *Male* pride.

She'd been vulnerable, she realized. The dinner, the wine, Chef Jerome, a carriage ride, walking in the snow. *Christmas.* He'd actually used Christmas to weaken her resolve. The very man who was threatening to destroy the holiday for children had practically seduced her in Seattle's winter wonderland. What she recognized now was that in those circumstances, she would've experienced the same emotions with just about any man.

As was her habit, K.O. weighed herself first thing and gasped when she saw she was up two pounds. That fabulous dinner had come at a price. Two pounds. K.O. had to keep a constant eye on her weight, unlike her sister. Zelda was naturally thin whereas K.O. wasn't. Her only successful strategy for maintaining her weight was to weigh herself daily and then make adjustments in her diet.

Even before she'd finished putting on her workout gear, the phone rang again. K.O. could always hope that it was a potential employer, but caller ID informed her it was her sister.

"Merry Christmas, Zelda," K.O. said. This was one small way to remind her that keeping Santa away from Zoe and Zara was fundamentally wrong.

"Did you get it?" Zelda asked excitedly. "Did you get Dr. Jeffries' autograph for me?"

"Ah . . ."

"You didn't, did you?" Zelda's disappointment was obvious.

"Not exactly."

"Did you even *talk* to him?" her sister pressed.

"Oh, yes, we did plenty of that." She recalled their conversation, thinking he might have manipulated that, too, in order to win her over to his side. The dark side, she thought grimly. Like Narnia without Aslan, and no Christmas.

A stunned silence followed. "Together. You and Dr. Jeffries were together?"

"We went to dinner. . . ."

"You went to dinner with Dr. Wynn Jeffries?" Awe became complete disbelief.

"Yes, at Chez Jerome." K.O. felt like a name-dropper but she couldn't help it. No one ate at Chez Jerome and remained silent.

Zelda gasped. "You're making this up and I don't find it amusing."

"I'm not," K.O. insisted. "LaVonne arranged it. Dinner was incredible. In fact, I gained two pounds."

A short silence ensued. "Okay, I'm sitting down and I'm listening really hard. You'd

78

better start at the beginning."

"Okay," she said. "I saw Wynn, Dr. Jeffries, in the French Café."

"I already know that part."

"I saw him again." K.O. stopped abruptly, thinking better of telling her sister about the confrontation and calling him names. Not that referring to him as Jim Carrey and Charles Dickens was especially insulting, but still . . . "Anyway, it's not important now."

"Why isn't it?"

"Well, Wynn and I agreed to put that unfortunate incident behind us and start over."

"Oh, my goodness, what did you do?" Zelda demanded. "What did you say to him? You didn't embarrass him, did you?"

K.O. bit her lip. "Do you want to hear about the dinner or not?"

"Yes! I want to hear *everything*."

K.O. then told her about cocktails at LaVonne's and her neighbor's connection with the famous chef. She described their dinner in lavish detail and mentioned the carriage ride. The one thing she didn't divulge was the kiss, which shot into her memory like a flaming dart, reminding her how weak she really was.

As if reading her mind, Zelda asked, "Did

he kiss you?"

"Zelda! That's private."

"He did," her sister said with unshakable certainty. "I can't believe it. Dr. Wynn Jeffries kissed my sister! You don't even like him."

"According to LaVonne I will soon bear his children."

"What!"

"Sorry," K.O. said dismissively. "I'm getting ahead of myself."

"Okay, okay, I can see this is all a big joke to you."

"Not really."

"I don't even know if I should believe you."

"Zelda, I'm your sister. Would I lie to you?"

"Yes!"

Unfortunately Zelda was right. "I'm not this time, I swear it."

Zelda hesitated. "Did you or did you not get his autograph?"

Reluctant though she was to admit it, K.O. didn't have any choice. "Not."

"That's what I thought." Zelda bade her a hasty farewell and disconnected the call.

Much as she hated the prospect, K.O. put on her sweats and headed for the treadmill, which she kept stored under her bed for emergencies such as this. If she didn't do something fast to get rid of those two pounds, they'd stick to her hips like putty and harden. Then losing them would be like chiseling them off with a hammer. This, at least, was her theory of weight gain and loss. Immediate action was required. With headphones blocking outside distractions, she dutifully walked four miles and quit only when she was confident she'd sweated off what she'd gained. Still, a day of reduced caloric intake would be necessary.

She showered, changed her clothes and had a cup of coffee with skim milk. She worked on the Mulcahys' Christmas letter, munching a piece of dry toast as she did. After that, she transcribed a few reports. At one o'clock LaVonne stopped by with a request.

"I need help," she said, stepping into K.O.'s condo. She carried a plate of cookies.

"Okay." K.O. made herself look away from the delectable-smelling cookies. Her stomach growled. All she'd had for lunch was a small container of yogurt and a glass of V8 juice.

"I hate to ask," LaVonne said, "but I wasn't sure where else to turn."

"LaVonne, I'd do anything for you. You

know that."

Her friend nodded. "Would you write my Christmas letter for me?"

"Of course." That would be a piece of cake. Oh, why did everything come down to food?

"I have no idea how to do this. I've never written one before." She sighed. "My life is pitiful."

K.O. arched her brows. "What do you mean, pitiful? You have a good life."

"I do? I've never married and I don't have children. I'm getting these Christmas letters from my old college friends and they're all about how perfect their lives are. In comparison mine is so dull. All I have are my three cats." She looked beseechingly at K.O. "Jazz up my life, would you? Make it sound just as wonderful as my girlfriends' instead of just plain boring."

"Your life is *not* boring." Despite her best efforts, K.O. couldn't keep her eyes off the cookies. "Would you excuse me?"

"Ah . . . sure."

"I'll be back in a minute. I need to brush my teeth."

Her neighbor eyed her speculatively as K.O. left the room.

"It's a trick I have when I get hungry," she explained, coming out of the bathroom holding her toothbrush, which was loaded with toothpaste. "Whenever I get hungry, I brush my teeth."

"You do what?"

"Brush my teeth."

Her friend regarded her steadily. "How many times have you brushed your teeth today?"

"Four . . . no, five times. Promise me you'll take those cookies home."

LaVonne nodded. "I brought them in case I needed a bribe."

"Not only will I write your letter, I'll do it today so you can mail off your cards this week."

Her friend's eyes revealed her gratitude. "You're the best."

Ideas were already forming in K.O.'s mind. Writing LaVonne's Christmas letter would be a snap compared to finishing Bill Mulcahy's. Speaking of him . . . K.O. glanced at her watch. She was scheduled to meet him this very afternoon.

"I've got an appointment at three," she told her friend. "I'll put something together for you right away, drop it off, see Bill and then stop at your place on my way back."

"Great." LaVonne was still focused on the toothbrush. "You're meeting Wynn later?"

She nodded. "At six." She should be

contacting him and canceling, but she didn't know how to reach him. It was a weak excuse — since she could easily ask LaVonne for his number. Actually, she felt it was time to own up to the truth. She wanted to see Wynn again, just so she'd have some answers. *Was* she truly attracted to him? *Did* he have some nefarious agenda, with the intent of proving himself right and her wrong? Unless she spent another evening with him, she wouldn't find out.

"Are you . . ." LaVonne waved her hand in K.O.'s direction.

"Am I what?"

LaVonne sighed. "Are you going to take that toothbrush with you?"

"Of course."

"I see." Her neighbor frowned. "My psychic vision didn't tell me anything about that."

"No, I don't imagine it would." K.O. proceeded to return to the bathroom, where she gave her teeth a thorough brushing. Perhaps if Wynn saw her foaming at the mouth, he'd know her true feelings about him.

CHAPTER 6

K.O. had fun writing LaVonne's Christmas letter. Compared to Bill Mulcahy's, it was a breeze. Her friend was worried about how other people, people from her long-ago past, would react to the fact that she'd never married and lacked male companionship. K.O. took care of that.

Merry Christmas to my Friends, K.O. began for LaVonne. *This has been an exciting year as I juggle my time between Tom, Phillip and Martin, the three guys in my life. No one told me how demanding these relationships can be. Tom won my heart first and then I met Phillip and how could I refuse him? Yes, there's a bit of jealousy, but they manage to be civil to each other. I will admit that things heated up after I started seeing Martin. I fell for him the minute we met.*

I'm retired now, so I have plenty of time to devote to the demands of these relationships. Some women discover love in their twenties.

But it took me until I was retired to fall into this kind of happiness. I lavish attention and love on all three guys. Those of you who are concerned that I'm taking on too much, let me assure you — I'm woman enough to handle them.

I love my new luxury condo on Blossom Street here in Seattle. And I've been continuing my education lately, enhancing my skills and exploring new vistas.

K.O. giggled, then glanced at her watch. The afternoon had escaped her. She hurriedly finished with a few more details of LaVonne's year, including a wine-tasting trip to the Yakima Valley, and printed out a draft of the letter.

The meeting with Bill Mulcahy went well, and he paid her the balance of what he owed and thanked her profusely. "This is just perfect," he said, reading the Christmas letter. "I wouldn't have believed it, if I wasn't seeing it for myself. You took the mess this year has been and turned it all around."

K.O. was pleased her effort had met with his satisfaction.

LaVonne was waiting for her when she returned, the Christmas letter in hand. "Oh, Katherine, I don't know how you do it. I laughed until I had tears in my eyes. How can I ever thank you?"

"I had fun," she assured her neighbor.

"I absolutely insist on paying you."

"Are you kidding? No way." After everything LaVonne had done for her, no thanks was necessary.

"I love it so much, I've already taken it down to the printer's and had copies made on fancy Christmas paper. My cards are going out this afternoon, thanks to you."

K.O. shrugged off her praise. After all, her friend had paid for her dinner with Wynn at Chez Jerome and been a good friend to her all these months. Writing a simple letter was the least she could do.

K.O. had been home only a short while when her doorbell chimed. Thinking it must be LaVonne, who frequently stopped by, she casually opened it, ready to greet her neighbor.

Instead Wynn Jeffries stood there.

K.O. wasn't ready for their outing — or to see him again. She needed to steel herself against the attraction she felt toward him.

"Hi." She sounded breathless.

"Katherine."

"Hi," she said again unnecessarily.

"I realize I'm early," he said. "I have a radio interview at 5:30. My assistant arranged it earlier in the week and I forgot to enter it into my PDA."

"Oh." Here it was — the perfect excuse to avoid seeing him again. And yet she couldn't help feeling disappointed.

He must've known, as she did, that any kind of relationship was a lost cause.

"That's fine, I understand," she told him, recovering quickly. "We can get together another time." She offered this in a nonchalant manner, shrugging her shoulders, deciding this really was for the best.

His gaze held hers. "Perhaps you could come with me," he said.

"Come with you?" she repeated and instantly recognized this as a bad idea. In fact, as bad ideas went, it came close to the top. She hadn't been able to keep her mouth shut in the bookstore and been banned for life. If she had to listen to him spout off his views in person, K.O. didn't know if she could restrain herself from grabbing the mike and pleading with people everywhere to throw out his book or use it for kindling. Nope, attending the interview with him was definitely *not* a good plan.

When she didn't immediately respond, he said, "After the interview, we could go on to the Figgy Pudding thing you mentioned."

She knew she should refuse. And yet,

before she could reconsider it, she found herself nodding.

"I understand the radio station is only a few blocks from West Lake Plaza."

"Yes . . ." Her mouth felt dry and all at once she was nervous.

"We'll need to leave right away," he said, looking at his watch.

"I'll get my coat." She was wearing blue jeans and a long black sweater — no need to change.

Wynn entered her condo and as she turned away, he stopped her, placing one hand on her arm.

K.O. turned back and was surprised to find him staring at her again. He seemed to be saying he wasn't sure what was happening between them, either. Wasn't sure what he felt or why . . . Then, as if he needed to test those feelings, he lowered his mouth to hers. Slowly, ever so slowly . . . K.O. could've moved away at any point. She didn't. The biggest earthquake of the century could've hit and she wouldn't have noticed. Not even if the building had come tumbling down around her feet. Her eyes drifted shut and she leaned into Wynn, ready — no, more than ready — *eager* to accept his kiss.

To her astonishment, it was even better

than the night before. This *couldn't* be happening and yet it was. Fortunately, Wynn's hands were on her shoulders, since her balance had grown unsteady.

When he pulled away, it took her a long time to open her eyes. She glanced up at him and discovered he seemed as perplexed as she was.

"I was afraid of that," he said.

She blinked, understanding perfectly what he meant. "Me, too."

"It was as good as last night."

"Better," she whispered.

He cleared his throat. "If we don't leave now, I'll be late for the interview."

"Right."

Still, neither of them moved. Apparently all they were capable of doing was staring at each other. Wynn didn't seem any happier about this than she was, and in some small way, that was a comfort.

K.O. forced herself to break the contact between them. She collected her coat and purse and was halfway to the door when she dashed into the bathroom. "I forgot my toothbrush," she informed him.

He gave her a puzzled look. "You brush after every meal?" he asked.

"No, before." She smiled sheepishly. "I mean, I didn't yesterday, which is why I have to do it today."

He didn't question her garbled explanation as she dropped her toothbrush carrier and toothpaste inside her purse.

Once outside the building, Wynn walked at a fast pace as if he already had second thoughts. For her part, K.O. tried not to think at all. To protect everyone's peace of mind, she'd decided to wait outside the building. It was safer that way.

By the time they arrived at the radio station, K.O. realized it was far too frigid to linger out in the cold. She'd wait in the lobby.

Wynn pressed his hand to the small of her back and guided her through the impressive marble-floored lobby toward the elevators.

"I'll wait here," she suggested. But there wasn't any seating or coffee shop. If she stayed there, it would mean standing around for the next thirty minutes or so.

"I'm sure they'll have a waiting area up at the station," Wynn suggested.

He was probably right.

They took the elevator together, standing as far away from each other as possible, as though they both recognized the risk for potential disaster.

The interviewer, Big Mouth Bass, was a well-known Seattle disk jockey. K.O. had listened to him for years but this was the first time she'd seen him in person. He didn't look anything like his voice. For one thing, he was considerably shorter than she'd pictured and considerably . . . rounder. If she had the opportunity, she'd share her toothbrush trick with him. It might help.

"Want to sit in for the interview?" Big Mouth asked.

"Thank you, no," she rushed to say. "Dr. Jeffries and I don't necessarily agree and —"

"No way." Wynn's voice drowned hers out.

Big Mouth was no fool. K.O. might've imagined it, but she thought a gleam appeared in his eyes. He hosted a live interview show, after all, and a little controversy would keep things lively.

"I insist," Big Mouth said. He motioned toward the hallway that led to the control booth.

K.O. shook her head. "Thanks, anyway, but I'll wait out here."

"We're ready for Dr. Jeffries," a young woman informed the radio personality.

"I'll wait here," K.O. said again, and before anyone could argue, she practically threw herself into a chair and grabbed a magazine. She opened it and pretended to read, sighing with relief as Big Mouth led Wynn out of the waiting area. The radio in the room was tuned to the station, and a couple of minutes later, Big Mouth's booming voice was introducing Wynn.

"I have with me Dr. Wynn Jeffries," he began. "As many of you will recall, Dr. Jeffries' book, *The Free Child,* advocates letting a child set his or her own boundaries. Explain yourself, Dr. Jeffries."

"First, let me thank you for having me on your show," Wynn said, and K.O. was surprised by how melodic he sounded, how confident and sincere. "I believe," Wynn continued, "that structure is stifling to a child."

"*Any* structure?" Big Mouth challenged.

"Yes, in my opinion, such rigidity is detrimental to a child's sense of creativity and his or her natural ability to develop moral principles." Wynn spoke eloquently, citing example after example showing how structure had a negative impact on a child's development.

"No boundaries," Big Mouth repeated, sounding incredulous.

"As I said, a child will set his or her own."

Just listening to Wynn from her chair in the waiting room, K.O. had to sit on her hands.

"You also claim a parent should ignore inappropriate talk."

"Absolutely. Children respond to feedback and when we don't give them any, the undesirable action will cease."

Big Mouth asked a question now and then. Just before the break, he said, "You brought a friend with you this afternoon."

"Yes . . ." All the confidence seemed to leave Wynn's voice.

"She's in the waiting area, isn't she?" Big Mouth continued, commenting more than questioning. "I gathered, during the few minutes in which I spoke to your friend, that she doesn't agree with your child-rearing philosophy."

"Yes, that's true, but Katherine isn't part of the interview."

Big Mouth chuckled. "I thought we'd bring her in after the break and get her views on your book."

"Uh . . ."

"Don't go away, folks — this should be interesting. We'll be right back after the traffic and weather report."

On hearing this, K.O. tossed aside the magazine and started to make a run for the elevator. Unfortunately Big Mouth was faster than his size had led her to believe.

"I . . . I don't think this is a good idea,"

she said as he led her by the elbow to the control booth. "I'm sure Wynn would rather not . . ."

"Quite the contrary," Big Mouth said smoothly, ushering her into the recording room, which was shockingly small. He sat her next to Wynn and handed her a headset. "You'll share a mike with Dr. Jeffries. Be sure to speak into it and don't worry about anything."

After the traffic report, Big Mouth was back on the air.

"Hello, Katherine," he said warmly. "How are you this afternoon?"

"I was perfectly fine until a few minutes ago," she snapped.

Big Mouth laughed. "Have you read Dr. Jeffries' book?"

"No. Well, not really." She leaned close to the microphone.

"You disagree with his philosophies, don't you?"

"Yes." She dared not look at Wynn, but she was determined not to embarrass him the way she had in the French Café. Even if they were at odds about the validity of his Free Child movement, he didn't deserve to be publicly humiliated.

"Katherine seems to believe I'm taking Christmas away from children," Wynn blurted out. "She's wrong, of course. I have a short chapter in the book that merely suggests parents bury the concept of Santa."

"You want to *bury Santa?*" Even Big Mouth took offense at that, K.O. noticed with a sense of righteousness.

"My publisher chose the chapter title and against my better judgment, I let it stand. Basically, all I'm saying is that it's wrong to lie to a child, no matter how good one's intentions."

"He wants to get rid of the Tooth Fairy and the Easter Bunny, too," K.O. inserted.

"That doesn't make me a Jim Carrey," Wynn said argumentatively. "I'm asking parents to be responsible adults. That's all."

"What does it hurt?" K.O. asked. "Childhood is a time of make-believe and fairy tales and fun. Why does everything have to be so serious?"

"Dr. Jeffries," Big Mouth cut in. "Could you explain that comment about Jim Carrey?"

"I called him that," K.O. answered on his behalf. "I meant to say the Grinch. You know, like in *The Grinch Who Stole Christmas.* Jim Carrey was in the movie," she explained helplessly.

Wynn seemed eager to change the subject. He started to say something about the macabre character of fairy tales and how they weren't "fun," but Big Mouth cut him off.

"Ah, I see," he said, grinning from ear to ear. "You two have a love/hate relationship. That's what's *really* going on here."

K.O. looked quickly at Wynn, and he glared back. The "hate" part might be right, but there didn't seem to be any "love" in the way he felt about her.

"Regrettably, this is all the time we have for today," Big Mouth told his audience. "I'd like to thank Dr. Jeffries for stopping by this afternoon and his friend Katherine, too. Thank you both for a most entertaining interview. Now for the news at the top of the hour."

Big Mouth flipped a switch and the room went silent. So silent, in fact, that K.O. could hear her heart beat.

"We can leave now," Wynn said stiffly after removing his headphones.

Hers were already off. K.O. released a huge pent-up sigh. "Thank goodness," she breathed.

Wynn didn't say anything until they'd entered the elevator.

"That was a disaster," he muttered.

K.O. blamed herself. She should never have accompanied him to the interview.

She'd known it at the time and still couldn't resist. "I'm sorry. I shouldn't have gone on the air with you."

"You weren't given much choice," he said in her defense.

"I apologize if I embarrassed you. That wasn't my intention. I tried not to say anything derogatory — surely you could see that."

He didn't respond and frankly, she didn't blame him.

"The thing is, Katherine, you don't respect my beliefs."

"I don't," she reluctantly agreed.

"You couldn't have made it any plainer." The elevator doors opened and they stepped into the foyer.

"Perhaps it would be best if we didn't see each other again." K.O. figured she was only saying what they were both thinking.

Wynn nodded. She could sense his regret, a regret she felt herself.

They were outside the building now. The street was festive with lights, and Christmas music could be heard from one of the department stores. At the moment, however, she felt anything but merry.

The Figgy Pudding contest, which was sponsored by the Pike Market Senior Center and Downtown Food Bank as an annual fund-raiser, would've started by now and, although she didn't feel the least bit like cheering, she'd promised Vickie she'd show up and support her efforts for charity.

K.O. thrust out her hand and did her utmost to smile. "Thank you, Wynn. Last night was one of the most incredible evenings of my life," she said. "Correction. It was *the* most incredible night ever."

Wynn clasped her hand. His gaze held hers as he said, "It was for me, too."

People were stepping around them.

She should simply walk away. Vickie would be looking for her. And yet . . . she couldn't make herself do it.

"Goodbye," he whispered.

Her heart was in her throat. "Goodbye."

He dropped his hand, turned and walked away. His steps were slow, measured. He'd gone about five feet when he glanced over his shoulder. K.O. hadn't moved. In fact, she stood exactly as he'd left her, biting her lower lip — a habit she had when distressed. Wynn stopped abruptly, his back still to her.

"Wynn, listen," she called and trotted toward him. "I have an idea." Although it'd only been a few feet, she felt as if she was setting off on a marathon.

"What?" He sounded eager.

"I have twin nieces."

He nodded. "You mentioned them earlier. Their mother read my book."

"Yes, and loved it."

There was a flicker of a smile. "At least *someone* in your family believes in me."

"Yes, Zelda sure does. She thinks you're fabulous." K.O. realized she did, too — aside from his theories. "My sister and her husband are attending his company Christmas dinner next Friday, the fifteenth," she rushed to explain. "Zelda asked me to spend the night. Come with me. Show me how your theories *should* work. Maybe Zelda's doing it wrong. Maybe you can convince me that the Free Child movement makes sense."

"You want me to come with you."

"Yes. We'll do everything just as you suggest in your book, and I promise not to say a word. I'll read it this week, I'll listen to you and I'll observe."

Wynn hesitated.

"Until then, we won't mention your book or anything else to do with your theories."

"Promise?"

"Promise," she concurred.

"No more radio interviews?"

She laughed. "That's an easy one."

A smile came to him then, appearing in his eyes first. "You've got yourself a deal."

Yes, she did, and K.O. could hardly wait to introduce Zoe and Zara to Dr. Wynn Jeffries. Oh, she was sincere about keeping an open mind, but Wynn might learn something, too. The incorrigible twins would be the true crucible for his ideas.

K.O. held out her hand. "Are you ready for some Figgy Pudding?" she asked.

He grinned, taking her mittened hand as they hurried toward the Figgy Pudding People's Choice competition.

CHAPTER 7

The Figgy Pudding People's Choice event was standing room only when Wynn and K.O. arrived. Vickie and her friends hadn't performed yet and were just being introduced by a popular morning-radio host for an easy-listening station. K.O. and Vickie had been friends all through high school and college. Vickie had married three years ago, and K.O. had been in her wedding party. In fact, she'd been in any number of wedding parties. Her mother had pointedly asked whether K.O. was ever going to be a bride, instead of a bridesmaid.

"That's my friend over there," K.O. explained, nodding in Vickie's direction. "The one in the Santa hat."

Wynn squinted at the group of ladies huddled together in front of the assembly. "Aren't they all wearing Santa hats?"

"True. The young cute one," she qualified.

"They're all young and cute, Katherine." He smiled. "Young enough, anyway."

She looked at Wynn with new appreciation. "That is such a sweet thing to say." Vickie worked for a local dentist as a hygienist and was the youngest member of the staff. The other women were all in their forties and fifties. "I could just kiss you," K.O. said, snuggling close to him. She looped her arm through his.

Wynn cleared his throat as though unaccustomed to such open displays of affection. "Any particular reason you suddenly find me so kissable?"

"Well, yes, the women with Vickie are . . . a variety of ages."

"I see. I should probably tell you I'm not wearing my glasses."

K.O. laughed, elbowing him in the ribs. "And here I thought you were being so gallant."

He grinned boyishly and slid his arm around her shoulders.

Never having attended a Figgy Pudding event before, K.O. didn't know what to expect. To her delight, it was enchanting, as various groups competed, singing Christmas carols, to raise funds for the Senior Center and Food Bank. Vickie and her office mates took second place, and K.O. cheered loudly.

Wynn shocked her by placing two fingers in his mouth and letting loose with a whistle that threatened to shatter glass. It seemed so unlike him.

Somehow Vickie found her when the singing was over. "I wondered if you were going to show," she said, shouting to be heard above the noise of the merry-go-round and the crowd. Musicians gathered on street corners, horns honked and the sights and sounds of Christmas were everywhere. Although the comment was directed at K.O., Vickie's attention was unmistakably on Wynn.

"Vickie, this is Wynn Jeffries."

Her friend's gaze shot back to K.O. "Wynn Jeffries? Not *the* Wynn Jeffries?"

"One and the same," K.O. said, speaking out of the corner of her mouth.

"You've got to be joking." Vickie's mouth fell open as she stared at Wynn.

For the last two months, K.O. had been talking her friend's ear off about the man and his book and how he was ruining her sister's life. She'd even told Vickie about the incident at the bookstore, although she certainly hadn't confided in anyone else; she wasn't exactly proud of being kicked out for unruly behavior. Thinking it might be best to change the subject, K.O. asked,

"Is John here?"

"John?"

"Your husband," K.O. reminded her. She hadn't seen Wynn wearing glasses before, but she hoped his comment about forgetting them was sincere, otherwise he might notice the close scrutiny Vickie was giving him.

"Oh, *John*," her friend said, recovering quickly. "No, he's meeting me later for dinner." Then, as if inspiration had struck, she asked, "Would you two like to join us? John got a reservation at a new Chinese restaurant that's supposed to have great food."

K.O. looked at Wynn, who nodded. "Sure," she answered, speaking for both of them. "What time?"

"Nine. I was going to do some shopping and meet him there."

They made arrangements to meet later and Vickie went into the mall to finish her Christmas shopping.

"I'm starving now," K.O. said when her stomach growled. Although she had her toothbrush, there really wasn't a convenient place to foam up. "After last night, I didn't think I'd ever want to eat again." She considered mentioning the two pounds she'd gained, but thought better of it. Wynn might not want to see her again if he found out how easily she packed on weight. Well, she didn't *really* believe that of him, but she wasn't taking any chances. Which proved that, despite everything, she was interested. In fact, she'd made the decision to continue with this relationship, see where their attraction might lead, almost without being aware of it.

"How about some roasted chestnuts?" he asked. A vendor was selling them on the street corner next to a musician who strummed a guitar and played a harmonica at the same time. His case was open on the sidewalk for anyone who cared to donate. She tossed in a dollar and hoped he used whatever money he collected to pay for music lessons.

"I've never had a roasted chestnut," K.O. told him.

"Me, neither," Wynn confessed. "This seems to be the season for it, though."

While Wynn waited in line for the chestnuts, K.O. became fascinated with the merry-go-round. "Will you go on it with me?" she asked him.

Wynn hesitated. "I've never been on a merry-go-round."

K.O. was surprised. "Then you have to," she insisted. "You've missed a formative experience." Taking his hand, she pulled him out of the line. She purchased the tickets herself and refused to listen to his excuses. He rattled off a dozen — he was too old, too big, too clumsy and so on. K.O. rejected every one.

"It's going to be fun," she said.

"I thought you were starving."

"I was, but I'm not now. Come on, be a good sport. Women find men who ride horses extremely attractive."

Wynn stopped arguing long enough to raise an eyebrow. "My guess is that the horse is generally not made of painted wood."

"Generally," she agreed, "but you never know."

The merry-go-round came to a halt and emptied out on the opposite side. They passed their tickets to the attendant and, leading Wynn by the hand, K.O. ushered him over to a pair of white horses that stood side by side. She set her foot in the stirrup and climbed into the molded saddle. Wynn stood next to his horse looking uncertain.

"Mount up, partner," she said.

"I feel more than a little ridiculous, Katherine."

"Oh, don't be silly. Men ride these all the time. See? There's another guy."

Granted, he was sitting on a gaudy elephant, holding a toddler, but she didn't dwell on that.

Sighing, Wynn climbed reluctantly onto the horse, his legs so long they nearly touched the floor. "Put your feet in the stirrups," she coaxed.

He did, and his knees were up to his ears.

K.O. couldn't help it; she burst out laughing.

Wynn began to climb off, but she stopped him by leaning over and kissing him. She nearly slid off the saddle in the process and would have if Wynn hadn't caught her about the waist.

Soon the carousel music started, and the horses moved up and down. K.O. thrust out her legs and laughed, thoroughly enjoying herself. "Are you having fun yet?" she asked Wynn.

"I'm ecstatic," he said dryly.

"Oh, come on, Wynn, relax. Have some fun."

Suddenly he leaned forward, as if he were riding for the Pony Express. He let out a cry that sounded like sheer joy.

"That *was* fun," Wynn told her, climbing down when the carousel stopped. He put his hands on her waist and she felt the heat of his touch in every part of her body.

"You liked it?"

"Do you want to go again?" he asked.

The line was much longer now. "I don't think so."

"I've always wanted to do that. I felt like a child all over again," he said enthusiastically.

"A Free Child?" she asked in a mischievous voice.

"Yes, free. That's exactly what my book's about, allowing children freedom to become themselves," he said seriously.

"Okay." She was biting her tongue but managed not to say anything more. Surely there were great rewards awaiting her in heaven for such restraint.

"Would you like to stop at the bookstore?" he asked. "I like to sign copies when I'm in the neighborhood."

"You mean an autographing?" She hoped it wouldn't be at the same bookstore that had caused all the trouble.

"Not exactly an autographing," Wynn explained. "The bookseller told me that a signed book is a sold book. When it's convenient, authors often visit bookstores to sign stock."

"Sort of a drive-by signing?" she asked, making a joke out of it.

"Yeah." They started walking and just as she feared, they were headed in the direction of *the* bookstore.

As they rounded the corner and the store came into sight, her stomach tightened. "I'll wait for you outside," she said, implying that nothing would please her more than to linger out in the cold.

"Nonsense. There's a small café area where you can wait in comfort."

"Okay," she finally agreed. Once she'd made it past the shoplifting detector K.O. felt more positive. She was afraid her mug shot had been handed out to the employees and she'd be expelled on sight.

Thankfully she didn't see the bookseller who'd asked her to leave. That boded well. She saw Wynn chatting with a woman behind the counter. He followed her to the back of the store. Some of the tension eased from K.O.'s shoulder blades. Okay, she seemed to be safe. And she didn't have to hide behind a coffee cup. Besides, she loved to read and since she was in a bookstore, what harm would it do to buy a book? She was in the mood for something entertaining. A romantic comedy, she decided, studying a row of titles. Without much trouble, she found one that looked perfect and started toward the cashier.

Then it happened.

Wynn was waiting up front, speaking to

the very bookseller who'd banished K.O. from the store.

Trying to be as inconspicuous as possible, K.O. set the book aside and tiptoed toward the exit, shoulders hunched forward, head lowered.

"Katherine," Wynn called.

With a smile frozen in place, she turned to greet Wynn and the bookseller.

"It's you!" The woman, who wore a name tag that identified her as Shirley, glared at K.O.

She timidly raised her hand. "Hello again."

"You two know each other?" Shirley asked Wynn in what appeared to be complete disbelief.

"Yes. This is my friend Katherine."

The bookseller seemed to have lost her voice. She looked from Wynn to Katherine and then back.

"Good to see you again," K.O. said. She sincerely hoped Shirley would play along and conveniently forget that unfortunate incident.

"It *is* you," Shirley hissed from between clenched teeth.

"What's this about?" Wynn asked, a puzzled expression on his face. "You've met before?"

"Nothing," K.O. all but shouted.

"As a matter of fact, we have met." Shirley's dark eyes narrowed. "Perhaps your *friend* has forgotten. I, however, have not."

So it was going to be like that, was it? "We had a difference of opinion," K.O. told Wynn in a low voice.

"As I recall, you were permanently banned from the store."

"Katherine was *banned* from the store?" Wynn asked incredulously. "I can't believe she'd do anything deserving of that."

"Maybe we should leave now," K.O. suggested, and tugged at his sleeve.

"If you want to know," Shirley began, but K.O. interrupted before she could launch into her complaint.

"Wynn, please, we should go," she said urgently.

"I'm sure this can all be sorted out," he murmured, releasing his coat sleeve from her grasp.

Shirley, hands on her hips, smiled snidely. She seemed to take real pleasure in informing Wynn of K.O.'s indiscretion.

"This *friend* of yours is responsible for causing a scene in this very bookstore, Dr. Jeffries."

"I'm sure no harm was meant."

K.O. grabbed his arm. "It doesn't matter," she said, desperate to escape.

"Katherine does tend to be opinionated, I agree," he said, apparently determined to defend her. "But she's actually quite reasonable."

"Apparently you don't know her as well as you think."

"I happen to enjoy Katherine's company immensely."

Shirley raised her eyebrows. "Really?"

"Yes, really."

"Then you might be interested to know that your so-called friend nearly caused a riot when she got into an argument with another customer over *your* book."

Wynn swiveled his gaze to K.O.

She offered him a weak smile. "Ready to leave now?" she asked in a weak whisper.

CHAPTER 8

K.O.'s doorbell chimed, breaking into a satisfying dream. Whatever it was about seemed absolutely wonderful and she hated to lose it. When the doorbell rang again, the sound longer and more persistent, the dream disappeared. She stumbled out of bed and threw on her flannel housecoat.

Reaching the door, she checked the peep-hole and saw that it was LaVonne. No surprise there. Unfastening the lock, K.O. let her in, covering a yawn.

"What time did you get home last night?" her neighbor cried as she hurried in without a cat — which was quite unusual. "I waited up as long as I could for you." LaVonne's voice was frantic. "I didn't sleep a wink all night," she said and plopped herself down on the sofa.

K.O. was still at the front door, holding it open. "Good morning to you, too."

"Should I make coffee?" LaVonne asked,

leaping to her feet and flipping on the light as she swept into the kitchen. Not waiting for a response, she pulled out the canister where K.O. kept her coffee grounds.

K.O. yawned again and closed the front door. "What time is it?" Early, she knew, because her eyes burned and there was barely a hint of daylight through her living room windows.

"Seven-twenty. I didn't get you up, did I?"

"No, I had to answer the door anyway." Her friend was busy preparing coffee and didn't catch the joke. "How are the guys?" K.O. asked next. LaVonne usually provided her with daily updates on their health, well-being and any cute activities they'd engaged in.

"They're hiding," she said curtly. "All three of them." She ran water into the glass pot and then poured it in the coffeemaker.

Katherine wondered why the cats were in a snit but didn't have the energy to ask.

"You haven't answered my question," LaVonne said as the coffee started to drip. She placed two mugs on the counter.

"Which one?" K.O. fell into a kitchen chair, rested her arms on the table and leaned her head on them.

"Last night," LaVonne said. "Where were you?"

"Wynn and I were out —"

"*All* night?"

"You're beginning to sound like my mother," K.O. protested.

LaVonne straightened her shoulders. "Katherine, you hardly know the man."

"I didn't sleep with him, if that's what you think." She raised her head long enough to speak and then laid it down on her arms again. "We went out to dinner with some friends of mine after the Figgy Pudding contest."

"It must've been a very late dinner." LaVonne sounded as if she didn't quite believe her.

"We walked around for a while afterward and went out for a drink. The time got away from us. I didn't get home until one."

"I was up at one and you weren't home," LaVonne said in a challenging tone. She poured the first cup of coffee and took it herself.

"Maybe it was after two, then," K.O. said. She'd completely lost track of time, which was easy to do. Wynn was so charming and he seemed so interested in her and her friends.

Vickie's husband, John, was a plumbing

116

contractor. Despite Wynn's college degrees and celebrity status, he'd fit in well with her friends. He'd asked intelligent questions, listened and shared anecdotes about himself that had them all laughing. John even invited Wynn to play poker with him and his friends after the holidays. Wynn had accepted the invitation.

Halfway through the meal Vickie had announced that she had to use the ladies' room. The look she shot K.O. said she should join her, which K.O. did.

"That's really Wynn Jeffries?" she asked, holding K.O.'s elbow as they made their way around tables and through the restaurant.

"Yes, it's really him."

"Does he know about the bookstore?"

K.O. nodded reluctantly. "He does now."

"You didn't tell him, did you?"

"Unfortunately, he found out all on his own."

Vickie pushed open the door to the ladies' as K.O. described the scene from the bookstore. "No way," her friend moaned, then promptly sank down on a plush chair in the outer room.

K.O.'s face grew red all over again. "It was embarrassing, to say the least."

"Was Wynn upset?"

What could he say? "He didn't let on if he was." In fact, once they'd left the store, Wynn seemed to find the incident highly amusing. Had their roles been reversed, she didn't know how she would've felt.

"He didn't blow up at you or anything?" Vickie had given her a confused look. "This is the guy you think should be banned from practicing as a psychologist?"

"Well, that might've been a bit strong," she'd said, reconsidering her earlier comment.

Vickie just shook her head.

"He rode the merry-go-round with me," K.O. said aloud, deciding that had gone a long way toward redeeming him in her eyes. When she glanced up, she realized she was talking to LaVonne.

"He did what?" LaVonne asked, bringing her back to the present.

"Wynn did," she elaborated. "He rode the carousel with me."

"Until two in the morning?"

"No, before dinner. Afterward, we walked along the waterfront, then had a glass of wine. We started walking again and finally stopped for coffee at an all-night diner and talked some more." He seemed to want to know all about her, but in retrospect she noticed that he'd said very little about himself.

"Good grief," LaVonne muttered, shaking her head, "what could you possibly talk about for so long?"

"That's just it," K.O. said. "We couldn't *stop* talking." And it was even more difficult to stop kissing and to say good-night once they'd reached her condo. Because there was so much more to say, they'd agreed to meet for coffee at the French Café at nine.

LaVonne had apparently remembered that Katherine didn't have any coffee yet and filled her mug. "Just black," K.O. told her, needing a shot of unadulterated caffeine. "Thanks."

"Why were you waiting up for me?" she asked after her first bracing sip of coffee. Then and only then did her brain clear, and she understood that LaVonne must have something important on her mind.

"You wrote that fantastic Christmas letter for me," her neighbor reminded her.

"I did a good job, didn't I?" she said.

"Oh, yes, a good job all right." LaVonne frowned. "I liked it so much, I mailed it right away."

"So, what's the problem?"

"Well . . ." LaVonne sat down in the chair across from K.O. "It was such a relief to have something clever and . . . and exciting to tell everyone," LaVonne said, "especially my college friends."

So far, K.O. didn't see any problem at all. She nodded, encouraging her friend to get to the point.

LaVonne's shoulders sagged. "If only I'd waited," she moaned. "If only I'd picked up my own mail first."

"There was something in the mail?"

LaVonne nodded. "I got a card and a Christmas letter from Peggy Solomon. She was the president of my college sorority and about as uppity as they come. She married her college boyfriend, a banker's son. She had two perfect children and lives a life of luxury. She said she's looking forward to seeing me at our next reunion." There was a moment of stricken silence. "Peggy's organizing it, and she included the invitation with her card."

"That's bad?"

"Yes," LaVonne wailed. "It's bad. How am I supposed to show up at my forty-year college reunion, which happens to be in June, without a man? Especially *now*. Because of my Christmas letter, everyone in my entire class will think I've got more men than I know what to do with."

"LaVonne, you might meet someone

before then."

"If I haven't met a man in the last forty years, what makes you think I will in the next six months?"

"Couldn't you say it's such a tricky balancing act you don't dare bring any of them?"

LaVonne glared at her. "Everyone'll figure out that it's all a lie." She closed her eyes. "And if they don't, Peggy's going to make sure she tells them."

Another idea struck K.O. "What about your psychic powers? Why don't you go check out the litter box again?" On second thought, maybe that wasn't such a great idea.

"Don't you think I would if I could?" she cried, becoming ever more agitated. "But I don't see anything about myself. Trust me, I've tried. So far, all my insights have been about you and Wynn. A lot of good my new-found talent has done *me.* You're being romanced night and day, and I've just made a complete fool of myself."

"LaVonne . . ."

"Even my cats are upset with me."

"Tom, Phillip and Martin?" K.O. had never understood why her neighbor couldn't name her feline companions regular cat names like Fluffy or Tiger.

"They think *I'm* upset with *them*. They're all hiding from me, and that's never happened before."

K.O. felt guilty, but she couldn't have known about the college reunion, any more than LaVonne did. "I'm sure everything will work out for the best," she murmured. She wished she had more than a platitude to offer, but she didn't.

"At this point that's all I can hope for." LaVonne expelled her breath and took another sip of coffee. That seemed to relax her, and she gave K.O. a half smile. "Tell me about you and Wynn."

"There's not much to say." And yet there was. She honestly liked him. Vickie and John had, too. Never would K.O. have guessed that the originator of the Free Child Movement she so reviled would be this warm, compassionate and genuinely nice person. She would've been happy to settle for *one* of those qualities. Despite everything K.O. had done to embarrass him, he was attracted to her. And it went without saying that she found Wynn Jeffries compelling and smart and . . . wonderful. But she was afraid to examine her feelings too closely — and even more afraid to speculate about his.

"You've spent practically every minute of the last two days together," LaVonne said.

122

"There's got to be something."

Shrugging, K.O. pushed her hair away from her face.

"You were with him until two this morning."

"And I'm meeting him at the café in about an hour and a half," she said as she glanced at the time on her microwave.

"So what gives?" LaVonne pressed.

"I like him," she said simply. K.O. hadn't been prepared to have any feelings for him, other than negative ones. But they got along well — as long as they didn't discuss his book.

Overjoyed by her confession, LaVonne clapped her hands. "I knew it!"

K.O. felt it would be wrong to let her friend think she really believed in this psychic nonsense. She'd cooperated with LaVonne's fantasy at first but now it was time to be honest. "Wynn said he asked you about me before you introduced us."

LaVonne looked away. "He did, but it was just in passing."

"He knew I lived in the building and had seen me around."

Her neighbor shifted in her seat. She cleared her throat before answering. "All right, all right, I was aware that he might be interested." She paused. "He asked me if you were single."

Really? Wynn hadn't told her that. "When was this?"

"Last week."

"Was it before or after you discovered your psychic talents?"

"Before."

Ah-ha.

"Why didn't he just introduce himself?"

"I asked him that, too," LaVonne said. "Apparently he's shy."

"Wynn?"

LaVonne raised one shoulder. She frowned over at the phone on the counter. "You've got a message."

It'd been so late when she finally got to bed that K.O. hadn't bothered to check. Reaching over, she pressed the Play button.

"K.O.," Zelda's voice greeted her. "Good grief, where are you? You don't have a date, do you?" She made it sound as if that was the last thing she expected. "Is there any chance it's with Dr. Jeffries? Call me the minute you get home." The message was followed by a lengthy beep and then there was a second message.

"Katherine," Zelda said more forcefully this time. "I don't mean to be a pest, but I'd appreciate it if you'd get back to me as soon as possible. You're out with Dr. Jeffries, aren't you?" Zelda managed to make that sound both accusatory and improbable.

Another beep.

"In case you're counting, this is the third time I've phoned you tonight. Where can you possibly be this late?"

No one ever seemed to care before, K.O. thought, and now her sister and LaVonne were suddenly keeping track of her love life.

Zelda gave a huge sigh of impatience. "I won't call again. But I need to confirm the details for Friday night. You're still baby-sitting, aren't you?"

"I'll be there," K.O. muttered, just as if her sister could hear. *And so will Wynn.*

Zelda added, "And I'd really like it if you'd get me that autograph."

"I will, I will," K.O. promised. She figured she'd get him to sign Zelda's copy of his book on Friday evening.

LaVonne drained the last of her coffee and set the mug in the sink. "I'd better get back. I'm going to try to coax the boys out from under the bed," she said with a resigned look as she walked to the door.

"Everything'll work out," K.O. assured her again — with a confidence she didn't actually feel.

LaVonne responded with a quick wave and left, slamming the door behind her.

Now K.O. was free to have a leisurely shower, carefully choose her outfit . . . and daydream about Wynn.

CHAPTER 9

Wynn had already secured a window table when K.O. arrived at the French Café. As usual, the shop was crowded, with a long line of customers waiting to place their orders.

In honor of the season, she'd worn a dark-blue sweater sprinkled with silvery stars and matching star earrings. She hung her red coat on the back of her chair.

Wynn had thoughtfully ordered for her, and there was a latte waiting on the table, along with a bran muffin, her favorite. K.O. didn't remember mentioning how much she enjoyed the café's muffins, baked by Alix Townsend, who sometimes worked at the counter. The muffins were a treat she only allowed herself once a week.

"Good morning," she said, sounding a little more breathless than she would've liked. In the space of a day, she'd gone from distrust to complete infatuation. Just twenty-four hours ago, she'd been inventing ways to get out of seeing Wynn again, and now . . . now she could barely stand to be separated from him.

She broke off a piece of muffin, after a sip of her latte in its oversize cup. "How did you know I love their bran muffins?" she asked. The bakery made them chock-full of raisins and nuts, so they were deliciously unlike blander varieties. Not only that, K.O. always felt she'd eaten something healthy when she had a bran muffin.

"I asked the girl behind the counter if she happened to know what you usually ordered, and she recommended that."

Once again proving how thoughtful he was.

"You had one the day you were here talking to some guy," he said flippantly.

"That was Bill Mulcahy," she explained. "I met with him because I wrote his Christmas letter."

Wynn frowned. "He's one of your clients?"

"I told you how I write people's Christmas letters, remember?" It'd been part of their conversation the night before. "I'll write yours if you want," she said, and then thinking better of it, began to sputter a retraction.

She needn't have worried that he'd take

her up on the offer because he was already declining. He shook his head. "Thanks, anyway." He grimaced. "I don't want to offend you, but I find that those Christmas letters are typically a pack of lies!"

"Okay," she said mildly. She decided not to argue. K.O. sipped her coffee again and ate another piece of muffin, deciding not to worry about calories, either. "Don't you just love Christmas?" she couldn't help saying. The sights and sounds of the season were all around them. The café itself looked elegant; garlands draped the windows and pots of white and red poinsettias were placed on the counter. Christmas carols played, just loudly enough to be heard. A bell-ringer collecting for charity had set up shop outside the café and a woman sat at a nearby table knitting a Christmas stocking. K.O. had noticed a similar one displayed in A Good Yarn, the shop across the street, the day she'd followed Wynn. Christmas on Blossom Street, with its gaily decorated streetlights and cheerful banners, was as Christmassy as Christmas could be.

"Yes, but I had more enthusiasm for the holidays before today," Wynn said.

"What's wrong?"

He stared down at his dark coffee. "My father left a message on my answering machine last night." He hesitated as he glanced up at her. "Apparently he's decided — at the last minute — to join me for Christmas."

"I see," she said, although she really didn't. Wynn had only talked about his parents that first evening, at Chez Jerome. She remembered that his parents had been hippies, and that his mother had died and his father owned a company that manufactured surfboard wax. But while she'd rattled on endlessly about her own family, he'd said comparatively little about his.

"He didn't bother to ask if I had other plans, you'll notice," Wynn commented dryly.

"Do you?"

"No, but that's beside the point."

"It must be rather disconcerting," she said. Parents sometimes did things like that, though. Her own mother often made assumptions about holidays, but it had never troubled K.O. She was going to miss her parents this year and would've been delighted if they'd suddenly decided to show up.

"Now I have to go to the airport on Sunday and pick him up." Wynn gazed out the window at the lightly falling snow. "As you might've guessed, my father and I have a rather . . . difficult relationship."

"I'm sorry." She wasn't sure what to say.

"The thing is," Wynn continued. "My father's like a big kid. He'll want to be entertained every minute he's here. He has no respect for my work or the fact that I have to go into the office every day." Wynn had told her he met with patients most afternoons; he kept an office in a medical building not far from Blossom Street.

"I'm sorry," she said again.

Wynn accepted her condolences with a casual shrug. "The truth is, I'd rather spend my free time with you."

He seemed as surprised by this as K.O. herself. She sensed that Wynn hadn't been any more prepared to feel this way about her than she did about him. It was all rather unexpected and at the same time just plain wonderful.

"Maybe I can help," K.O. suggested. "The nice thing about working at home is that I can choose my own hours." That left her open for job interviews, Christmas letters and occasional baby-sitting. "My transcription work is really a godsend while I'm on my job quest. So I can help entertain him if you'd like."

Wynn considered for a moment. "I appreciate your offer, but I don't know if that's the best solution." He released a deep sigh. "I guess you could say my father's not my biggest fan."

"He doesn't believe in your child-rearing ideas, either?" she teased.

He grinned. "I wish it was that simple. You'll know what I mean once you meet him," Wynn said. "I think I mentioned that at one time he was a world-class surfer."

"Yes, and he manufactures some kind of special wax."

Wynn nodded. "It's made him rich." He sighed again. "I know it's a cliché, but my parents met in San Francisco in the early 70s and I think I told you they joined a commune. They were free spirits, the pair of them. Dad hated what he called 'the establishment.' He dropped out of college, burned his draft card, that sort of thing. He didn't want any responsibility, didn't even have a bank account — until about fifteen years ago, when someone offered to mass-produce his surfboard wax. And then he grabbed hold with both hands."

K.O. wondered if he realized he was advocating his parents' philosophy with his Free Child Movement. However, she didn't point it out.

"In the early days we moved around because any money Dad brought in was from his surfing, so the three of us followed the waves, so to speak. Then we'd periodically return to the commune. I had a wretched childhood," he said bleakly. "They'd called me Radiant Sun, Ray for short, but at least they let me choose my own name when I was older. They hated it, which was fine by me. The only real family I had was my maternal grandparents. I moved in with the Wynns when I was ten."

"Your parents didn't like your name?"

"No, and this came from someone who chose the name Moon Puppy for himself. Mom liked to be called Daffodil. Her given name was Mary, which she'd rejected, along with her parents' values."

"But you —"

"My grandparents were the ones who saw to it that I stayed in school. They're the ones who paid for my education. Both of them died when I was a college senior, but they were the only stable influence I had."

"What you need while your father is here," K.O. said, "is someone to run interference. Someone who can act as a buffer between you and your father, and that someone is me."

Wynn didn't look convinced.

"I want to help," she insisted. "Really."

He still didn't look convinced.

"Oh, and before I forget, my sister left three messages on my phone. She wants your autograph in the worst way. I thought you could sign her copy of *The Free Child* next Friday when —" It suddenly occurred to her that if Wynn's father was visiting, he wouldn't be able to watch the twins with her. "Oh, no," she whispered, unable to hide her disappointment.

"What's wrong?"

"I — You'll have company, so Friday night is out." She put on a brave smile. She didn't actually need his help, but this was an opportunity to spend time with him — and to prove that his theories didn't translate into practice. She might be wrong, in which case she'd acknowledge the validity of his Free Child approach, but she doubted it.

Wynn met her eyes. "I'm not going to break my commitment. I'll explain to my father that I've got a previous engagement. He doesn't have any choice but to accept it, especially since he didn't give me any notice."

"When does he arrive?" K.O. asked. She savored another piece of her muffin, trying to guess which spices Alix had used.

"At four-thirty," Wynn said glumly.

"It's going to work out fine." That was almost identical to what she'd told LaVonne earlier that morning.

Then it hit her.

LaVonne needed a man in her life.

Wynn was looking for some way to occupy his father.

"Oh, my goodness." K.O. stood and stared down at Wynn with both hands on the edge of the table.

"What?"

"Wynn, I have the perfect solution!"

He eyed her skeptically.

"LaVonne," she said, sitting down again. She was so sure her plan would work, she felt a little shiver of delight. "You're going to introduce your father to LaVonne!"

He frowned at her and shook his head. "If you're thinking what I suspect you're thinking, I can tell you right now it won't work."

"Yes, it will! LaVonne needs to find a man before her college reunion in June. She'd —"

"Katherine, I appreciate the thought, but can you honestly see LaVonne getting involved with an ex-hippie who isn't all that ex — and is also the producer of Max's Wax?"

"Of course I can," she said, refusing to allow him to thwart her plan. "Besides, it isn't up to us. All we have to do is introduce the two of them, step back and let nature take its course."

Wynn clearly still had doubts.

"It won't hurt to try."

"I guess not . . ."

"This is what I'll do," she said, feeling inspired. She couldn't understand Wynn's hesitation. "I'll invite your father and LaVonne to my place for Christmas cocktails."

Wynn crossed his arms. "This is beginning to sound familiar."

"It should." She stifled a giggle. Turnabout was fair play, after all.

"Maybe we should look at the olives in the martinis and tell them we got a psychic reading," Wynn joked.

"Oh, that's good," K.O. said with a giggle. "A drink or two should relax them both," she added.

"And then you and I can conveniently leave for dinner or a movie."

"No . . . no," K.O. said, excitedly. "Oh, Wynn this is ideal! We'll arrange a dinner for *them*."

"Where?"

"I don't know." He was worrying about details too much. "We'll think of someplace special."

"I wonder if I can reach Chef Jerome and get a reservation there," Wynn murmured.

K.O. gulped. "I can't afford that."

"Not to worry. My father can."

"That's even better." K.O. felt inordinately pleased with herself. All the pieces were falling into place. Wynn would have someone to keep his father occupied until Christmas, and LaVonne might find a potential date for her class reunion.

"What are your plans for today?" Wynn asked, changing the subject.

"I'm meeting Vickie and a couple of other friends for shopping and lunch. What about you?"

"I'm headed to the gym and then the office. I don't usually work on weekends, but I'm writing a follow-up book." He spoke hesitantly as if he wasn't sure he should mention it.

"Okay." She smiled as enthusiastically as she could. "Would you like me to go to the airport with you when you pick up your father?"

"You'd do that?"

"Of course! In fact, I'd enjoy it."

"Thank you, then. I'd appreciate it."

They set up a time on Sunday afternoon and went their separate ways.

K.O. started walking down to Pacific Place, the mall where she'd agreed to meet Vickie and Diane, when her cell phone rang.

It was Wynn.

"What day?" he asked. "I want to get this cocktail party idea of yours on my schedule."

"When would you suggest?"

"I don't think we should wait too long."

"I agree."

"Would Monday evening work for you?"

"Definitely. I'll put together a few appetizers and make some spiked eggnog. I'll pick up some wine — and gin for martinis, if you want." She smiled, recalling his comment about receiving a "psychic" message from the olives.

"Let me bring the wine. Anything else?"

"Could you buy a cat treat or two? That's in case LaVonne brings Tom or one of her other cats. I want her to concentrate on Moon Puppy, not kitty."

Wynn laughed. "You got it. I'll put in a call to Chef Jerome, although I don't hold out much hope. Still, maybe he'll say yes because it's LaVonne."

"All we can do is try. And there are certainly other nice places."

Wynn seemed reluctant to end the conversation. "Katherine."

"Yes."

"Thank you. Hearing my father's message after such a lovely evening put a damper on my Christmas."

"You're welcome."

"Have fun today."

"You, too." She closed her cell and set it back in her purse. Her step seemed to have an extra bounce as she hurried to meet her friends.

CHAPTER 10

Saturday afternoon, just back from shopping, K.O. stopped at LaVonne's condo. She rang the doorbell and waited. It took her neighbor an unusually long time to answer; when she did, LaVonne looked dreadful. Her hair was disheveled, and she'd obviously been napping — with at least one cat curled up next to her, since her dark-red sweatshirt was covered in cat hair.

"Why the gloomy face?" K.O. asked. "It's almost Christmas."

"I know," her friend lamented.

"Well, cheer up. I have great news."

"You'd better come inside," LaVonne said without any real enthusiasm. She gestured toward the sofa, although it seemed to require all the energy she possessed just to lift her arm. "Sit down if you want."

"Wouldn't you like to hear my good news?"

LaVonne shrugged her shoulders. "I guess."

"It has to do with you."

"Me?"

"Yup. I met Vickie and Diane at Pacific Place, and we had lunch at this wonderful Italian restaurant."

LaVonne sat across from her, and Martin automatically jumped into her lap. Tom got up on the chair, too, and leisurely stretched out across the arm. She petted both cats with equal fondness.

"I ordered the minestrone soup," K.O. went on to tell her, maintaining her exuberance. "That was when it happened." She'd worked out this plan on her way home, inspired by Wynn's joke about the olives.

"What?"

"I had a psychic impression. Isn't that what you call it? Right there with my two friends in the middle of an Italian restaurant." She paused. "It had to do with romance."

"Really?" LaVonne perked up, but only a little.

"It was in the soup."

"The veggies?"

"No, the crackers," K.O. said and hoped she wasn't carrying this too far. "I crumbled them in the soup and —"

"What did you see?" Then, before K.O. could answer, LaVonne held out one hand. "No, don't tell me, let me guess. It's about you and Wynn," her neighbor said. "It must be."

"No . . . no. Remember how you told me you don't have the sight when it comes to yourself? Well, apparently I don't, either."

LaVonne looked up from petting her two cats. Her gaze narrowed. "What did you see, then?"

"Like I said, it was about *you*," K.O. said, doing her best to sound excited. "You're going to meet the man of your dreams."

"I am?" She took a moment to consider this before her shoulders drooped once more.

"Yes, you! I saw it plain as anything."

"Human or feline?" LaVonne asked in a skeptical voice.

"Human," K.O. announced triumphantly.

"When?"

"The crackers didn't say exactly, but I felt it must be soon." K.O. didn't want to tell LaVonne too much, otherwise she'd ruin the whole thing. If she went overboard on the details, her friend would suspect K.O. was setting her up. She needed to be vague, but still implant the idea.

"I haven't left my condo all day," LaVonne

mumbled, "and I don't plan to go out anytime in the near future. In fact, the way I feel right now, I'm going to be holed up in here all winter."

"You're overreacting."

Her neighbor studied her closely. "Katherine, you *really* saw something in the soup?"

"I did." Nothing psychic, but she wasn't admitting that. She'd seen elbow macaroni and kidney beans and, of course, the cracker crumbs.

"But you didn't take the class. How were you able to discover your psychic powers if you weren't there to hear the lecture from Madam Ozma?" she wanted to know.

K.O. crossed her fingers behind her back. "It must've rubbed off from spending all that time with you."

"You think so?" LaVonne asked hopefully.

"Sure." K.O. was beginning to feel bad about misleading her friend. She'd hoped to mention the invitation for Monday night, but it would be too obvious if she did so now.

"There might be something to it," LaVonne said, smiling for the first time. "You never know."

"True . . . one never knows."

"Look what happened with you and

143

Wynn," LaVonne said with a glimmer of excitement. "The minute I saw those two raisins gravitate toward each other, I knew it held meaning."

"I could see that in the crackers, too."

This was beginning to sound like a church revival meeting. Any minute, she thought, LaVonne might stand up and shout *Yes, I believe!*

"Then Wynn met you," she burbled on, "and the instant he did, I saw the look in his eyes."

What her neighbor had seen was horror. LaVonne couldn't have known about their confrontation earlier that day. He'd clearly been shocked and, yes, horrified to run into K.O. again. Especially with the memory of her ranting in the café so fresh in his mind.

"You're right," LaVonne said and sat up straighter. "I shouldn't let a silly letter upset me."

"Right. And really, you don't even know how much of what your college friend wrote is strictly true." K.O. remembered the letter she'd written for Bill Mulcahy. Not exactly lies, but not the whole truth, either.

"That could be," LaVonne murmured, but she didn't seem convinced. "Anyway, I know better than to look to a man for happiness." LaVonne was sounding more like her old self. "Happiness comes from within, isn't that right, Martin?" she asked, holding her cat up. Martin dangled from her grasp, mewing plaintively. "I don't need a man to be complete, do I?"

K.O. stood up, gathering her packages as she did. Toys and books for the twins, wrapping paper, a jar of specialty olives.

"Thanks for stopping by," LaVonne said when K.O. started toward the door. "I feel a hundred percent better already."

"Keep your eyes open now," she told LaVonne. "The man in the soup could be right around the corner." Or on the top floor of their condo building, she added silently.

"I will," her neighbor promised and, still clutching Martin, she shut the door.

Sunday afternoon Wynn came to K.O.'s door at three, his expression morose.

"Cheer up," she urged. "Just how bad can it be?"

"Wait until you meet Moon Puppy. Then you'll know."

"Come on, is your father really *that* bad?"

Wynn sighed deeply. "I suppose not. He's lonely without my mother. At loose ends."

"That's good." She paused, hearing what she'd said. "It's not good that he's lonely,

but . . . Well, you know what I mean."
LaVonne might seem all the more attractive
to him if he craved female companionship.
LaVonne deserved someone who needed
her, who would appreciate her and her cats
and her . . . psychic talents.

"You ready?" he asked.

"Let me grab my coat."

"You don't have to do this, you know."

"Wynn, I'm happy to," she assured him,
and she meant it.

The airport traffic was snarled, and it took
two turns through the short-term parking
garage to find an available space. Thankfully they'd allotted plenty of time.

Wynn had agreed to meet his father at
baggage claim. No more than five minutes
after they'd staked out a place near the lug-
gage carousel, a man wearing a Hawaiian
shirt, with long dark hair tied in a ponytail,
walked toward them. He didn't have a
jacket or coat.

K.O. felt Wynn stiffen.

"Wynn!" The man hurried forward.

Wynn met his father halfway, with K.O.
trailing behind, and briefly hugged him.
"Hello, Dad." He put his hand on K.O.'s
shoulder. "This is my friend Katherine
O'Connor. Katherine, this is my father,
Moon Puppy Jeffries."

Moon Puppy winced. "Delighted to meet you, Katherine," he said politely. "But please, call me Max. I don't go by Moon Puppy anymore."

"Welcome to Seattle," K.O. said, shaking hands. "I'm sorry you didn't arrive to sunshine and warmer weather."

"Thank you. Don't worry, I've got a jacket in my bag."

In a few minutes Max had collected his suitcase and Wynn led the way to his car. "It's been unseasonably chilly," K.O. said, making small talk as they took the escalator to the parking garage. Max had retrieved his jacket by then.

At the car, Wynn took the suitcase from his father and stored it in the trunk. This gave K.O. an opportunity to study father and son. She glanced at Wynn and then back at his father. After the description Wynn had given her, she'd expected something quite different. Yes, Max Jeffries looked like an old hippie, as Wynn had said, but his hair was neatly trimmed and combed. He wore clean, pressed clothes and had impeccable manners. He was an older version of Wynn and just as respectable looking, she thought. Well, except for the hair.

"It was a surprise to hear you were coming for Christmas," Wynn commented when he got into the car.

"I figured it would be," his father said. "I didn't mention it earlier because I was afraid you'd find a convenient excuse for me not to come."

So Max Jeffries was direct and honest, too. A lot like his son. K.O. liked him even more.

They chatted on the ride into Seattle, and K.O. casually invited him for cocktails the following afternoon.

"I'd enjoy that," Wynn's father told her.

"Katherine wants to introduce you to her neighbor, LaVonne."

"I see," Max said with less enthusiasm and quickly changed the subject. "I understand your book is selling nicely."

"Yes, I'm fortunate to have a lot of publisher support."

"He's writing a second book," K.O. said, joining the conversation. It pleased her that Max seemed proud of his son.

"So, how long have you two been seeing each other?" Max asked, looking at K.O.

"Not long," Wynn answered for them. His gaze caught K.O.'s in the rearview mirror. "We met through a psychic," he said.

"We most certainly did not." K.O. was about to argue when she realized Wynn was smiling. "We actually met through a mutual friend who believes she has psychic powers," she explained, not telling Max that her neighbor and this "psychic" were one and the same.

As they exited off the freeway and headed into downtown Seattle and toward Blossom Street, Max said, "I had no idea Seattle was this beautiful."

"Oh, just wait until nighttime," K.O. told him. It was fast becoming dark, and city lights had begun to sparkle. "There's lots to do at night. Wynn and I took a horse-drawn carriage ride last week and then on Friday night we went on a merry-go-round."

"My first such experience," Wynn said, a smile quivering at the edges of his mouth.

"Your mother and I never took you?" Max sounded incredulous.

"Never."

"I know I had some failings as a father," Max said despondently.

"Not getting to ride on a merry-go-round isn't exactly a big deal, Dad. Don't worry about it," Wynn muttered.

That seemed to ease his father's mind. "So what's on the agenda for tomorrow?" he asked brightly.

Wynn cast K.O. a look as if to say he'd told her so.

"I can take you on a tour of Pike Place

Market," K.O. offered.

"That would be great." Max thanked her with a warm smile. "I was hoping to get a chance to go up the Space Needle while I'm here, too."

"We can do that on Tuesday."

Max nodded. "Do you have any free time, Wynn?" he asked.

"Some," Wynn admitted with obvious reluctance. "But not much. In addition to my appointments and writing schedule, I'm still doing promotion for my current book."

"Of course," Max murmured.

K.O. detected a note of sadness in his voice and wanted to reassure him. Unfortunately she didn't know how.

CHAPTER 11

Wynn phoned K.O. early Monday morning. "I don't think this is going to work," he whispered.

"Pardon?" K.O. strained to hear.

"Meet me at the French Café," he said, his voice only slightly louder.

"When?" She had her sweats on and was ready to tackle her treadmill. After shedding the two pounds, she'd gained them again. It wasn't much, but enough to send her racing for a morning workout. She knew how quickly these things could get out of control.

"Now," he said impatiently. "Want me to pick you up?"

"No. I'll meet you there in ten minutes."

By the time she entered the café, Wynn had already purchased two cups of coffee and procured a table. "What's wrong?" she asked as she pulled out the chair.

"He's driving me insane!"

"Wynn, I like your father. You made him

sound worse than a deadbeat dad, but he's obviously proud of you and —"

"Do you mind if we don't list his admirable qualities just now?" He brought one hand to his temple, as if warding off a headache.

"All right," she said, doing her best to understand.

"The reason I called is that I don't think it's a good idea to set him up with LaVonne."

"Why not?" K.O. thought her plan was brilliant. She had everything worked out in her mind; she'd bought the liquor and intended to dust and vacuum this afternoon. As far as she was concerned, the meeting of Max and LaVonne was destiny. Christmas romances were always the best.

"Dad isn't ready for another relationship," Wynn declared. "He's still mourning my mother."

"Shouldn't he be the one to decide that?" Wynn might be a renowned child psychologist but she believed everyone was entitled to make his or her own decisions, especially in matters of the heart. She considered it all right to lend a helping hand, however. That was fair.

"I can tell my father's not ready," Wynn insisted.

"But I invited him for drinks this evening and he accepted." It looked as if her entire day was going to be spent with Max Jeffries, aka Moon Puppy. Earlier she'd agreed to take him to Pike Place Market, which was a must-see for anyone visiting Seattle. It was always an entertaining place for tourists, but never more so than during the holiday season. The whole market had an air of festivity, the holiday mood infectious.

"What about LaVonne?" he asked.

"I'll give her a call later." K.O. hadn't wanted to be obvious about this meeting. Still, when LaVonne met Max, she'd know, the same way Wynn and K.O. had known, that they were being set up.

"Don't," he said, cupping the coffee mug with both hands.

"Why not?"

He frowned. "I have a bad feeling about this."

K.O. smothered a giggle. "Are you telling me you've found your own psychic powers?"

"Hardly," he snorted.

"Wynn," she said, covering his hand with hers in a gesture of reassurance. "It's going to work out fine, trust me." Hmm. She seemed to be saying that a lot these days.

He exhaled slowly, as if it went against his

better judgment to agree. "All right, do whatever you think is best."

"I've decided to simplify things. I'm serving eggnog and cookies." And olives, if anyone wanted them. When she'd find time to bake she didn't know, but K.O. was determined to do this properly.

"Come around five-thirty," she suggested.

"That early?"

"Yes. You're taking care of arranging their dinner, right?"

"Ah . . . I don't think they'll get that far."

"But they might," she said hopefully. "You make the reservation, and if they don't want to go, then we will. Okay?"

He nodded. "I'll see what I can do." Wynn took one last swallow of coffee and stood. "I've got to get to the office." Slipping into his overcoat, he confided, "I have a patient this morning. Emergency call."

K.O. wondered what kind of emergency that would be — an ego that needed splinting? A bruised id? But she knew better than to ask. "Have a good day," was all she said. In his current mood, that was an iffy proposition. K.O. couldn't help wondering what Max had done to upset him.

"You, too," he murmured, then added, "And thank you for looking after Moon Puppy."

"His name is Max," K.O. reminded him.

"Maybe to you, but to me he'll always be the hippie surfer bum I grew up with." Wynn hurried out of the café.

By five that afternoon, K.O. felt as if she'd never left the treadmill. After walking for forty minutes on her machine, she showered, baked and decorated three dozen cookies and then met Wynn's father for a whirlwind tour of the Seattle waterfront, starting with Pike Place. She phoned LaVonne from the Seattle Aquarium. LaVonne had instantly agreed to drinks, and K.O. had a hard time getting off the phone. LaVonne chatted excitedly about the man in the soup, the man K.O. had claimed to see with her "psychic" eyes. Oh, dear, maybe this had gone a little too far. . . .

Max was interested in absolutely everything, so they didn't get back to Blossom Street until after four, which gave K.O. very little time to prepare for *the meeting.*

She vacuumed and dusted and plumped up the sofa pillows and set out a dish of peppermint candies, a favorite of LaVonne's. The decorated sugar cookies were arranged on a special Santa plate. K.O. didn't particularly like sugar cookies, which, therefore, weren't as tempting as shortbread or chocolate chip would've been. She decided against the olives.

K.O. was stirring the rum into the eggnog when she saw the blinking light on her phone. A quick check told her it was Zelda. She didn't have even a minute to chat and told herself she'd return the call later.

Precisely at 5:30 p.m., just after she'd put on all her Christmas CDs, Wynn arrived without his father. "Where's your dad?" K.O. demanded as she accepted the bottle of wine he handed her.

"He's never on time if there's an excuse to be late," Wynn muttered. "He'll get here when he gets here. You noticed he doesn't wear a watch?"

K.O. had noticed and thought it a novelty. LaVonne wasn't known for her punctuality, either, so they had at least that much in common. Already this relationship revealed promise — in her opinion, anyway.

"How did your afternoon go?" Wynn asked. He sat down on the sofa and reached for a cookie, nodding his head to the tempo of "Jingle Bell Rock."

"Great. I enjoyed getting to know your father."

Wynn glanced up, giving her a skeptical look.

"What is it with you two?" she asked

gently, sitting beside him.

Wynn sighed. "I didn't have a happy childhood, except for the time I spent with my grandparents. I resented being dragged hither and yon, based on where the best surf could be found. I hated living with a bunch of self-absorbed hippies whenever we returned to the commune, which was their so-called home base. For a good part of my life, I had the feeling I was a hindrance my father tolerated."

"Oh, Wynn." The unhappiness he still felt was at odds with the amusing stories he'd told about his childhood at Chez Jerome and during dinner with Vickie and John. She'd originally assumed that he was reflecting his own upbringing in his "Free Child" theories, but she now saw that wasn't the case. Moon Puppy Max might have been a hippie, but he'd imposed his own regimen on his son. Not much "freedom" there.

"Well, that's my life," he said stiffly. "I don't want my father here and I dislike the way he's using you and —"

"He's not using me."

He opened his mouth to argue, but apparently changed his mind. "I'm not going to let my father come between us."

"Good, because I'd feel terrible if that happened." This would be a near-perfect relationship — if it wasn't for the fact that he was Wynn Jeffries, author of *The Free Child*. And the fact that he hadn't forgiven his father, who'd been a selfish and irresponsible parent.

His eyes softened. "I won't let it." He kissed her then, and K.O. slipped easily into his embrace. He wrapped his arms around her and they exchanged a series of deep and probing kisses that left K.O.'s head reeling.

"Katherine." Wynn breathed harshly as he abruptly released her.

She didn't want him to stop.

"You'd better answer your door," he advised.

K.O. had been so consumed by their kisses that she hadn't heard the doorbell. "Oh," she breathed, shaking her head to clear away the fog of longing. This man did things to her heart — not to mention the rest of her — that even a romance novelist couldn't describe.

Wynn's father stood on the other side of the door, wearing another Hawaiian flowered shirt, khaki pants and flip-flops. From the way he'd dressed, he could be on a tropical isle rather than in Seattle with temperatures hovering just above freezing. K.O. could tell that Max's choice of clothes irritated Wynn, but to his credit, Wynn didn't comment.

Too bad the current Christmas song was "Rudolph," instead of "Mele Kaliki Maka."

K.O. welcomed him and had just poured his eggnog when the doorbell chimed again. Ah, the moment she'd been waiting for. Her friend had arrived. K.O. glided toward the door and swept it open as if anticipating Santa himself.

"LaVonne," she said, leaning forward to kiss her friend's cheek. "How good of you to come." Her neighbor had brought Tom with her. The oversize feline was draped over her arm like a large furry purse.

"This is so kind of you," LaVonne said. She looked startled at seeing Max.

"Come in, please," K.O. said, gesturing her inside. She realized how formal she sounded — like a character in an old drawing room comedy. "Allow me to introduce Wynn's father, Max Jeffries. Max, this is LaVonne Young."

Max stood and backed away from LaVonne. "You have a cat on your arm."

"This is Tom," LaVonne said. She glanced down lovingly at the cat as she stepped into the living room. "Would you like to say hello?" She held Tom out, but Max shook his head adamantly.

By now he'd backed up against the wall.

"I don't like cats."

"What?" She sounded shocked. "Cats are magical creatures."

"Maybe to you they are," the other man protested. "I don't happen to be a cat person."

Wynn shared an I-told-you-so look with K.O.

"May I get you some eggnog?" K.O. asked, hoping to rescue the evening from a less-than-perfect beginning.

"Please," LaVonne answered just as "Have Yourself a Merry Little Christmas" began.

Eager for something to do, K.O. hurried into the kitchen and grabbed the pitcher of eggnog.

She heard Tom hiss loudly and gulped down some of her own eggnog to relax.

"Your cat doesn't like me," Max said as he carefully approached the sofa.

"Oh, don't be silly. Tom's the friendly one."

"You mean you have *more* than one?"

"Dad," Wynn said, "why don't you sit down and make yourself comfortable. You're quite safe. Tom is very well-behaved."

"I don't like cats," Max reiterated.

"Tom is gentle and loving," LaVonne said.

Max slowly approached the sofa. "Then why is he hissing at me?"

"He senses your dislike," LaVonne explained. She gave Max a dazzling smile. "Pet him, and he'll be your friend for life."

"See, Dad?" Wynn walked over to LaVonne, who sat with Tom on her lap. He ran his hand down Tom's back and the tabby purred with pleasure.

"He likes you," Max said.

"He'll like you, too, as soon as you pet him," LaVonne was still smiling happily, stroking the cat's head.

Max came a bit closer. "You live in the building?" he asked, making his way, step by careful step, toward LaVonne.

"Just across the hall," she answered.

"Your husband, too?"

"I'm single. Do you enjoy cards? Because you're welcome to stop by anytime."

K.O. delivered the eggnog. This was going even better than she'd hoped. Max was already interested and LaVonne was issuing invitations. She recognized the gleam in the other man's eyes. A sense of triumph filled her and she cast a glance in Wynn's direction. Wynn was just reaching into his pocket, withdrawing a real-looking catnip mouse.

Relaxed now, Max leaned forward to pet Tom.

At that very moment, chaos broke out. Although LaVonne claimed she'd never known Tom to take a dislike to anyone, the cat clearly detested Max. Before anyone could react, he sprang from her lap and grabbed Max's bare arm. The cat's claws dug in, drawing blood. He wasn't about to let go, either.

"Get him off," Max screamed, thrashing his arm to and fro in an effort to free himself from the cat-turned-killer. Wynn was desperately — and futilely — trying to distract Tom by waving the toy mouse. It didn't help.

"Tom, Tom!" LaVonne screeched at the top of her lungs.

Blood spurted onto the carpet.

In a panic, Max pulled at Tom's fur. The cat then sank his teeth into Max's hand and Max yelped in pain.

"Don't hurt my cat," LaVonne shrieked.

Frozen to the spot, K.O. watched in horror as the scene unfolded. Wynn dropped the mouse, and if not for his quick action, K.O. didn't know what would have happened. Before she could fully comprehend how he'd done it, Wynn had disentangled Tom from his father's arm. LaVonne instantly took her beloved cat into her embrace and cradled him against her side.

At the sight of his own blood, Max looked like he was about to pass out. K.O. hurriedly got him a clean towel, shocked at the amount of blood. The scratches seemed deep. "Call 9-1-1," Max shouted.

Wynn pulled out his cell phone. "That might not be a bad idea," he said to K.O. "Cat scratches can get infected."

"Contact the authorities, too," Max added, glaring at LaVonne. He stretched out his good arm and pointed at her. "I want that woman arrested and her animal destroyed."

LaVonne cried out with alarm and hovered protectively over Tom. "My poor kitty," she whispered.

"You're worried about the *cat?*" Max said. "I'm bleeding to death and you're worried about your cat?"

Wynn replaced his phone. "The medics are on their way."

"Oh . . . good." K.O. could already hear sirens in the background. She turned off her CD player. Thinking she should open the lobby door, she left the apartment, and when the aid car arrived, she directed the paramedics. Things had gotten worse in the short time she was gone. Max and LaVonne were shouting at each other as the small living room filled with people. Curious onlookers crowded the hallway outside her door.

"My cat scratched him and I'm sorry, but

he provoked Tom," LaVonne said stubbornly.

"I want that woman behind bars." Max stabbed his finger in LaVonne's direction.

"Sir, sir, we need you to settle down," instructed the paramedic who was attempting to take his blood pressure.

"While she's in jail, declaw her cat," Max threw in.

Wynn stepped up behind K.O. "Yup," he whispered. "This is a match made in heaven, all right."

Then, just when K.O. was convinced nothing more could go wrong, her phone started to ring.

CHAPTER 12

"Don't you think you should answer that?" the paramedic treating Max's injuries asked.

K.O. was too upset to move. The romantic interlude she'd so carefully plotted couldn't have gone worse. At least Wynn seemed to understand her distress.

"I'll get it," Wynn said, and strode into the kitchen. "O'Connor residence," he said. At the way his eyes instantly shot to her, K.O. regretted not answering the phone herself.

"It's your sister," he said, holding the phone away from his ear.

Even above the racket K.O. could hear Zelda's high-pitched excitement. Her idol, Dr. Wynn Jeffries, had just spoken to her. The last person K.O. wanted to deal with just then was her younger sister. However, she couldn't subject Wynn to Zelda's adoration.

She took the phone, but even before she

had a chance to speak, Zelda was shrieking, "Is it *really* you, Dr. Jeffries? Really and truly?"

"Actually, no," K.O. informed her sister. "It's me."

"But Dr. Jeffries is with you?"

"Yes."

"Keep him there!"

"I beg your pardon?"

"Don't let him leave," Zelda said, sounding even more excited. "I'm calling on my cell. I'm only a few minutes away." She took a deep breath. "I need to talk to him. It's urgent. Zach and I just had the biggest argument *ever,* and I need to talk to Dr. Jeffries."

"Zelda," K.O. cut in. "Now is not the best time for you to visit."

"Didn't you hear me?" her sister cried. "This is an emergency."

With that, the phone went dead. Groaning, K.O. replaced the receiver.

"Is something wrong?" Wynn asked as he stepped around the paramedic who was still looking after Max.

"It's Zelda. She wants — no, *needs* — to talk to you. According to her it's an emergency." K.O. felt the need to warn him. "She's already on her way."

"Now? You mean she's coming now?"

K.O. nodded. "Apparently so." Zelda

hadn't mentioned what this argument with Zach was about. Three guesses said it had to do with Christmas and Wynn's theories. Oh, great. Her sister was arriving at the scene of a disaster.

"Are you taking him to the h-hospital?" LaVonne sobbed, covering her mouth with both hands.

"It's just a precaution," the medic answered. "A doctor needs to look at those scratches."

"Not that dreadful man!" LaVonne cried, pointing at Max. "I'm talking about my cat."

"Oh." The paramedic glanced at his companion. "Unfortunately, in instances such as this, we're obliged to notify Animal Control."

"You're hauling my Tom to . . . jail?"

"Quarantine," he told her gently.

For a moment LaVonne seemed about to faint. Wynn put his arm around the older woman's shoulders and led her to the sofa so she could sit down. "This can't be happening," LaVonne wailed. "I can't believe this is happening to my Tom."

"Your cat should be —"

Wynn cast his father a look meaningful enough to silence the rest of whatever Max had planned to say.

"I'm going to be scarred for life," Max

shouted. "I just hope you've got good insurance, because you're going to pay for this. And you're going to pay big."

"Don't you dare threaten me!" LaVonne had recovered enough to shout back.

With his arm stretched out in front of him, Max Jeffries followed the paramedic out of the condo and past the crowd of tenants who'd gathered in the hallway outside K.O.'s door.

"That . . . that terrible man just threatened me," LaVonne continued. "Tom's never attacked anyone like this before."

"Please, please, let me through."

K.O. heard her sister's voice.

Meanwhile LaVonne was weeping loudly. "My poor Tom. My poor, poor Tom. What will become of him?"

"What on earth is going on here?" Zelda demanded as she made her way into the apartment. The second paramedic was gathering up his equipment and getting ready to leave. The blood-soaked towels K.O. had wrapped around Max's arm were on the floor. The scene was completely chaotic and Zelda's arrival only added to the mayhem.

"Your f-father wants to s-sue me," LaVonne stuttered, pleading with Wynn. "*Do* something. Promise me you'll talk to him."

Wynn sat next to LaVonne and tried to comfort her. "I'll do what I can," he said. "I'm sure that once my father's settled down he'll listen to reason."

LaVonne's eyes widened, as though she had trouble believing Wynn. "I don't mean to insult you, but your father doesn't seem like a reasonable man to me."

"Whose blood is that?" Zelda asked, hands on her hips as she surveyed the room.

K.O. tried to waylay her sister. "As you can see," she said, gesturing about her, "this *really* isn't a good time to visit."

"I don't care," Zelda insisted. "I need to talk to Dr. Jeffries." She thrust his book at him and a pen. "Could you sign this for me?"

Just then a man wearing a jacket that identified him as an Animal Control officer came in, holding an animal carrier. The name Walt was embroidered on his shirt.

Wynn quickly signed his name, all the while watching the man from Animal Control.

LaVonne took one look at Walt and burst into tears. She buried her face in her hands and started to rock back and forth.

"Where's the cat?" Walt asked.

"We've got him in the bathroom," the paramedic said.

"Please don't hurt him," LaVonne wept. "Please, please . . ."

Walt raised a reassuring hand. "I handle situations like this every day. Don't worry, Miss, I'll be gentle with your pet."

"Dr. Jeffries, Dr. Jeffries." Zelda slipped past K.O. and climbed over LaVonne's knees in order to reach Wynn. She plunked herself down on the coffee table, facing him. "I really do need to talk to you."

"Zelda!" K.O. was shocked by her sister's audacity.

"Zach and I never argue," Zelda said over her shoulder, glaring at K.O. as if that fact alone should explain her actions. "This will only take a few minutes, I promise. Once I talk to Dr. Jeffries, I'll be able to tell Zach what he said and then he'll understand."

LaVonne wailed as Walt entered the bathroom.

K.O. heard a hiss and wondered if her shower curtain was now in shreds. She'd never seen a cat react to anyone the way Tom had to Wynn's father. Even now she couldn't figure out what had set him off.

"This'll only take a minute," Zelda went on. "You see, my husband and I read your book, and it changed everything. Well, to be perfectly honest, I don't know if Zach read the whole book." A frown crossed her face.

"LaVonne, perhaps I should take you home now," K.O. suggested, thinking it might be best for her neighbor not to see Tom leave the building caged.

"I can't leave," LaVonne said. "Not until I know what's happening to Tom."

The bathroom door opened and Walt reappeared with Tom safely inside the cat carrier.

"Tom, oh, Tom," LaVonne wailed, throwing her arms wide.

"Dr. Jeffries, Dr. Jeffries," Zelda pleaded, vying for his attention.

"Zelda, couldn't this wait a few minutes?" K.O. asked.

"Where are you taking Tom?" LaVonne demanded.

"We're just going to put him in quarantine," Walt said in a soothing voice.

"Tom's had all his shots. My veterinarian will verify everything you need to know."

"Good. Still, we're legally required to do this. I guarantee he'll be well looked after."

"Thank you," K.O. said, relieved.

"Can I speak to Dr. Jeffries now?" Zelda asked impatiently. "You see, I don't think my husband really did read your book," she continued, picking up where she'd left off. "If he had, we wouldn't be having this disagreement."

"I'll see LaVonne home," K.O. said. She closed one arm around her friend's waist and steered her out of the condo.

Wynn looked at Zelda and sent K.O. a beseeching glance.

"I'll be back as soon as I can," she promised.

He nodded and mouthed the word *hurry.*

K.O. rolled her eyes. As she escorted LaVonne, the sound of her sister's voice followed her into the hallway, which was fortunately deserted. It didn't take long to get LaVonne settled in her own place. Once she had Phillip and Martin with her, she was comforted, since both seemed to recognize her distress and lavished their mistress with affection.

When she returned to her condo, K.O. found that her sister hadn't moved. She still sat on the coffee table, so close to Wynn that their knees touched. Judging by the speed with which Zelda spoke, K.O. doubted he'd had a chance to get a word in edgewise.

"Then the girls started to cry," Zelda was saying. "They want a Christmas tree and Zach thinks we should get one."

"I don't believe —" Wynn was cut off before he could finish his thought.

"I know you don't actually condemn

Christmas trees, but I didn't want to encourage the girls about this Santa thing, and I feel decorating a tree would do that. If we're going to bury Santa under the sleigh — and I'm in complete agreement with you, Dr. Jeffries — then it makes sense to downplay everything else having to do with Christmas, too. Certainly all the commercial aspects. But how do I handle the girls' reaction when they hear their friends talking about Santa?"

Wynn raised a finger, indicating that he'd like to comment. His request, however, was ignored.

"I feel as you do," Zelda rushed on breathlessly, bringing one hand to her chest in a gesture of sincerity. "It's wrong to mislead one's children with figures of fantasy. It's wrong, wrong, wrong. Zach agreed with me — but only in principle, as it turns out. Then we got into this big fight over the Christmas tree and you have to understand that my husband and I hardly ever argue, so this is all very serious."

"Where's Zach now?" K.O. asked, joining Wynn on the sofa.

As if to let her know how much he appreciated having her back, Wynn reached for her hand. At Zelda's obvious interest, he released it, but the contact, brief as it was, reassured her.

Zelda lowered her head. "Zach's at home with the girls. If you must know, I sort of left my husband with the twins."

"Zoe and Zara," K.O. said under her breath for Wynn's benefit.

"Despite my strong feelings on the matter, I suspect my husband is planning to take our daughters out to purchase a Christmas tree." She paused. "A *giant* one."

"Do you think he might even decorate it with Santa figurines and reindeer?" K.O. asked, pretending to be scandalized.

"Oh, I hope not," Zelda cried. "That would ruin everything I've tried so hard to institute in our family."

"As I recall," Wynn finally said. He waited a moment as if to gauge whether now was a good time to insert his opinions. When no one interrupted him, he continued. "I didn't say anything in my book against Christmas trees, giant or otherwise."

"Yes, I know that, but it seems to me —"

"It seems to *me* that you've carried this a bit further than advisable," Wynn said gently. "Despite what you and K.O. think, I don't want to take Christmas away from your children or from you and your husband. It's a holiday to be celebrated. Family and traditions are important."

K.O. agreed with him. She felt gratified that there was common ground between them, an opinion on which they could concur. Nearly everything she'd heard about Wynn to this point had come from her sister. K.O. was beginning to wonder if Zelda was taking his advice to extremes.

"Besides," he said, "there's a fundamental contradiction in your approach. You're correct to minimize the element of fantasy — but your children are telling you what they want, aren't they? And you're ignoring that."

K.O. wanted to cheer. She took Wynn's hand again, and this time he didn't let go.

"By the way," Zelda said, looking from Wynn to K.O. and staring pointedly at their folded hands. "Just when did you two start dating?"

"I told you —"

"What you said," her sister broke in, "was that Dr. Jeffries lived in the same building as you."

"I told you we went to dinner a couple of times."

"You most certainly did not." Zelda stood up, an irritated expression on her face. "Well, okay, you did mention the one dinner at Chez Jerome."

"Did you know that I'm planning to join Katherine this Friday when she's watching the twins?" Wynn asked.

"She's bringing you along?" Zelda's eyes grew round with shock. "You might've said something to me," she burst out, clearly upset with K.O.

"I thought I had told you."

"You haven't talked to me in days," Zelda wailed. "It's like I'm not even your sister anymore. The last I heard, you were going to get Dr. Jeffries' autograph for me, and you didn't, although I specifically asked if you would."

"Would you prefer I not watch the twins?" Wynn inquired.

"Oh, no! It would be an honor," Zelda assured him, smiling, her voice warm and friendly. She turned to face K.O. again, her eyes narrowed. "But my own sister," she hissed, "should've told me she intended on having a famous person spend the night in my home."

"You're not to tell anyone," K.O. insisted.

Zelda glared at her. "Fine. I won't."

"Promise me," K.O. said. Wynn was entitled to his privacy; the last thing he needed was a fleet of parents in SUVs besieging him about his book.

"I promise." Without a further word, Zelda grabbed her purse and made a hasty exit.

"Zelda!" K.O. called after her. "I think we need to talk about this for a minute."

"I don't have a minute. I need to get home to my husband and children. We'll talk later," Zelda said in an ominous tone, and then she was gone.

CHAPTER 13

"I'd better leave now, as well," Wynn announced, getting his coat. "Dad'll need me to drive him back from the emergency room." K.O. was glad he didn't seem eager to go.

For her part, she wanted him to stay. Her nerves were frayed. Nothing had worked out as she'd planned and now everyone was upset with her. LaVonne, her dear friend, was inconsolable. Zelda was annoyed that K.O. hadn't kept her updated on the relationship with Wynn. Max Jeffries was just plain angry, and while the brunt of his anger had been directed at LaVonne, K.O. realized he wasn't pleased with her, either. Now Wynn had to go. Reluctantly K.O. walked him to the door. "Let me know how your father's doing, okay?" she asked, looking up at him.

"Of course." Wynn placed his hands on her shoulders. "You know I'd much rather be here with you."

She saw the regret in his eyes and didn't want to make matters worse. "Thank you for being so wonderful," she said and meant it. Wynn had been the voice of calm and reason throughout this entire ordeal.

"I'll call you about my father as soon as I hear."

"Thank you."

After a brief hug, he hurried out the door.

After a dinner of eggnog and peanut butter on crackers, K.O. waited up until after midnight, but no word came. Finally, when she couldn't keep her eyes open any longer, she climbed between the sheets and fell instantly asleep. This surprised her; she hadn't anticipated sleeping easily or well. When she woke the following morning, the first thoughts that rushed into her mind were of Wynn. Something must have happened, something unexpected and probably dreadful, or he would've called.

Perhaps the hospital had decided to keep Max overnight for observation. While there'd been a lot of blood involved, K.O. didn't think any of the cuts were deep enough to require stitches. But if Max had filed a police report, that would cause problems for LaVonne and might explain Wynn's silence. Every scenario that roared through her head pointed to trouble.

Even before she made her first cup of coffee, K.O.'s stomach was in knots. As she headed into the kitchen, she discovered a sealed envelope that had been slipped under her door.

It read:

Katherine,
I didn't get back from the hospital until late and I was afraid you'd already gone to bed. Dad's home and, other than being cantankerous, he's doing fine, so don't worry on his account. The hospital cleaned and bandaged his arm and said he'd be good as new in a week or so. Please reassure LaVonne. The cuts looked worse than they actually were.

Could you stop by my office this afternoon? I'm at the corner of Fourth and Willow, Suite 1110. Does one o'clock work for you? If you can't fit it into your schedule, please contact my assistant and let her know. Otherwise, I'll look forward to seeing you, then.

Wynn

Oh, she could fit it in. She could *definitely* fit it in. K.O. was ready to climb Mount Rainier for a chance to see Wynn. With purpose now, she showered and dressed and then, on the off-chance Max might need something, she phoned Wynn's condo.

His father answered right away, which made her wonder if he'd been sitting next to the phone waiting for a call.

"Good morning," she said, striving to sound cheerful and upbeat — all the while hoping Max wasn't one to hold grudges.

"Who is this?"

"It's K.O.," she told him, her voice faltering despite her effort to maintain a cheery tone.

He hesitated as if he needed time to place who she might be. "Oh," he finally said. "The woman from downstairs. The woman whose *friend* caused me irreparable distress." After another pause, he said, "I'm afraid I might be suffering from trauma-induced amnesia."

"Excuse me?" K.O. was sure she'd misunderstood.

"I was attacked yesterday by a possibly rabid beast and am fortunate to be alive. I don't remember much after that vicious animal sank its claws into my arm," he added shakily.

K.O. closed her eyes for a moment. "I'm so sorry to hear that," she said, going along

181

with it. "But the hospital released you, I see."

"Yes." This was said with disdain; apparently, he felt the medical profession had made a serious error in judgment. "I'm on heavy pain medication."

"Oh, dear."

"I don't know where my son's gone," he muttered fretfully.

If Wynn hadn't told his father he was at the office, then K.O. wasn't about to, either. She suspected Wynn had good reason to escape.

"Since you live in the building . . ." Max began.

"Uh . . ." She could see it coming. Max wanted her to sit and hold his uninjured hand for the rest of the day.

"I do, but unfortunately I'm on my way out."

"Oh."

It took K.O. a few more minutes to wade through the guilt he was shoveling in her direction. "I'll drop by and check on you later," she promised.

"Thank you," he said, ending their conversation with a groan, a last shovelful of guilt.

K.O. hung up the phone, groaning, too. This was even worse than she'd imagined and she had a fine imagination. Max was obviously playing this incident for all it was worth. Irreparable distress. Rabid beast. Trauma-induced amnesia! Oh, brother.

Wanting to leave before Max decided to drop by, she hurried out the door and stopped at the French Café for a mocha and bran muffin. If ever she'd deserved one, it was now. At the rate her life was going, there wouldn't be enough peppermint mochas in the world to see her through another day like yesterday.

Rather than linger as she normally did, K.O. took her drink and muffin to go and enjoyed a leisurely stroll down Blossom Street. A walk would give her exercise and clear her mind, and just then clarity was what she needed. She admired the evergreen boughs and garlands decorating the storefronts, and the inventive variations on Christmas themes in every window. The weather remained unseasonably cold with a chance of snow flurries. In December Seattle was usually in the grip of gloomy winter rains, but that hadn't happened yet this year. The sky was already a clear blue with puffy clouds scattered about.

By the time she'd finished her peppermint mocha, K.O. had walked a good mile and felt refreshed in both body and mind. When she entered her building, LaVonne — wearing a housecoat — was stepping out of her condo to grab the morning paper. Her eyes were red and puffy and it looked as if she hadn't slept all night. She bent over to retrieve her paper.

"LaVonne," K.O. called out.

Her friend slowly straightened. "I thought I should see if there's a report in the police blotter about Tom scratching that . . . that man," she spat out.

"I doubt it."

"Is he . . . back from the hospital?"

"Max Jeffries is alive and well. He sustained a few scratches, but it isn't nearly as bad as we all feared." Wynn's father seemed to be under the delusion that he'd narrowly escaped with his life, but she didn't feel the need to mention that. Nor did K.O. care to enlighten LaVonne regarding Max's supposed amnesia.

"I'm so glad." LaVonne sounded tired and sad.

"Is there anything I can get you?" K.O. asked, feeling partially to blame.

"Thanks for asking, but I'm fine." She gave a shuddering sob. "Except for poor Tom being in jail . . ."

"Call if you need me," K.O. said before she returned to her own apartment.

The rest of the morning passed quickly.

She worked for a solid two hours and accomplished more in that brief time than she normally did in four. She finished a medical report, sent off some résumés by e-mail and drafted a Christmas letter for a woman in Zach's office who'd made a last-minute request. Then, deciding she should check on Max Jeffries, she went up for a quick visit. At twelve-thirty, she grabbed her coat and headed out the door again. With her hands buried deep in her red wool coat and a candy-cane striped scarf doubled around her neck, she walked to Wynn's office.

This was her first visit there, and she wasn't sure what to expect. When she stepped inside, she found a comfortable waiting room and thought it looked like any doctor's office.

A middle-aged receptionist glanced up and smiled warmly. "You must be Katherine," she said, extending her hand. "I'm Lois Church, Dr. Jeffries' assistant."

"Hello," K.O. said, returning her smile.

"Come on back. Doctor is waiting for you." Lois led her to a large room, lined with bookshelves and framed degrees. A big desk dominated one end, and there was a sitting area on the other side, complete with a miniature table and chairs and a number of toys.

Wynn stood in front of the bookcase, and when K.O. entered the room, he closed the volume he'd been reading and put it back in place.

Lois slipped quietly out of the room and shut the door.

"Hi," K.O. said tentatively, wondering at his mood.

He smiled. "I see you received my note."

"Yes," she said with a nod. She remained standing just inside his office.

"I asked you to come here to talk about my father. I'm afraid he's going a little overboard with all of this."

"I got that impression myself."

Wynn arched his brows. "You've spoken to him?"

She nodded again. "I stopped by to see how he's doing. He didn't seem to remember me right away. He says he's suffering from memory loss."

Wynn groaned.

"I hate to say this, but I assumed that hypochondria's what he's really suffering from." She paused. "Either that or he's faking it," she said boldly.

Wynn gave a dismissive shrug. "I believe your second diagnosis is correct. It's a recurring condition of his," he said with a wry smile.

K.O. didn't know quite what to say.

"He's exaggerating, looking for attention." Wynn motioned for her to sit down, which she did, sinking into the luxurious leather sofa. Wynn took the chair next to it. "I don't mean to sound unsympathetic, but for all his easygoing hippie ways, Moon Puppy — Max — can be quite the manipulator."

"Well, it's not like LaVonne did it on purpose or anything."

There was a moment's silence. "In light of what happened yesterday, do you still want me to accompany you to your sister's?" he asked.

K.O. would be terribly disappointed if he'd experienced a change of heart. "I hoped you would, but if you need to bow out because of your father, I understand."

"No," he said decisively. "I want to do this. It's important for us both, for our relationship."

K.O. felt the same way.

"I've already told my father that I have a business appointment this weekend, so he knows I'll be away."

That made K.O. smile. This *was* business. Sort of.

"I'd prefer that Max not know the two of us will be together. He'll want to join us and, frankly, dealing with him will be more work than taking care of the kids."

"All right." Despite a bit of residual guilt, K.O. was certainly willing to abide by his wishes. She was convinced that once Wynn spent time with Zoe and Zara, he'd know for himself that his theories didn't work. The twins and their outrageous behavior would speak more eloquently than she ever could.

"I'm afraid we might not have an opportunity to get together for the rest of the week."

She was unhappy about it but understood. With his injuries and need for attention, Max would dominate Wynn's time.

"Are you sure your father will be well enough by Friday for you to leave?" she asked.

"He'd better be," Wynn said firmly, "because I'm going. He'll survive. In case you hadn't already figured this out, he's a little . . . immature."

"Really?" she asked, feigning surprise. Then she laughed out loud.

Wynn smiled, too. "I'm going to miss you, Katherine," he said with a sigh. "I wish I could see you every day this week, but between work and Max . . ."

"I'll miss you, too."

Wynn checked his watch and K.O. realized that was her signal to go. Wynn had appointments.

They both stood.

"Before I forget," he said casually. "A friend of mine told me his company's looking for a publicist. It's a small publisher, Apple Blossom Books, right in the downtown area, not far from here."

"They are?" K.O.'s heart raced with excitement. A small publishing company would be ideal. "Really?"

"I mentioned your name, and Larry asked if you'd be willing to send in a résumé." Wynn picked up a business card from his desk and handed it to her. "You can e-mail it directly to him."

"Oh, Wynn, thank you." In her excitement, she hugged him.

That seemed to be all the encouragement he needed to keep her in his arms and kiss her. She responded with equal fervor, and it made her wonder how she could possibly go another three days until she saw him again.

They smiled at each other. Wynn threaded his fingers through her hair and brought his mouth to hers for another, deeper kiss.

A polite knock at the door was followed by the sound of it opening.

Abruptly Wynn released her, taking a step

back. "Yes, Lois," he said, still looking at K.O.

"Your one-thirty appointment has arrived."

"I'll be ready in just a minute," he said. As soon as the door was shut, he leaned close, touching his forehead to hers. "I'd better get back to work."

"Me, too." But it was with real reluctance that they drew apart.

As K.O. left, glancing at the surly teen being ushered into his office, she felt that Friday couldn't come soon enough.

Chapter 14

On Thursday afternoon, LaVonne invited
K.O. for afternoon tea, complete with a
plate of sliced fruitcake. "I'm feeling much
better," her neighbor said as she poured tea
into mugs decorated with cats in Santa
costumes. "I've been allowed to visit Tom,
and he's doing so well. In a couple of days,
he'll be back home where he belongs." She
frowned as if remembering Wynn's father.
"No thanks to that dreadful man who had
Tom taken away from me."

K.O. sat on the sofa and held her mug in
one hand and a slice of fruitcake in the
other. "I'm so pleased to hear Tom will be
home soon." Her conscience had been
bothering her, and for the sake of their
friendship, K.O. felt the need to confess
what she'd done.

"The best part is I haven't seen that
maniac all week," LaVonne was saying.

K.O. gave her neighbor a tentative smile

and lowered her gaze. She hadn't seen Max, either. Or Wynn, except for that brief visit to his office, although they'd e-mailed each other a couple of times. He'd kept her updated on his father and the so-called memory loss, from which Max had apparently made a sudden recovery. In fact, he now remembered a little too much, according to Wynn. But the wounds on his arm appeared to be healing nicely and Max seemed to enjoy the extra attention Wynn paid him. Wynn, meanwhile, was looking forward to the reprieve offered by their visit to Zelda's.

"I owe you an apology," K.O. said to LaVonne.

"Nonsense. You had no way of knowing how Tom would react to Mr. Jeffries."

"True, but . . ." She swallowed hard. "You should know . . ." She started again. "I didn't really have a psychic experience."

LaVonne set down her mug and stared at K.O. "You didn't actually see a man for me in the soup? You mean to say there *wasn't* any message in the cracker crumbs?"

"No," K.O. admitted.

"Oh."

"It might seem like I was making fun of you and your psychic abilities, but I wasn't, LaVonne, I truly wasn't. I thought that if you believed a man was coming into your life, you'd be looking for one, and if you were expecting to meet a man, then you just might, and I hoped that man would be Wynn's father, but clearly it wasn't . . . isn't." This was said without pausing for breath.

A short silence ensued, followed by a disappointed, "Oh."

"Forgive me if I offended you."

LaVonne took a moment to think this through. "You didn't," she said after a while. "I've more or less reached the same conclusion about my psychic abilities. But —" she smiled brightly "— guess what? I've signed up for another class in January." She reached for a second slice of fruitcake and smiled as Martin brought K.O. the catnip mouse Wynn had given Tom that ill-fated evening.

"Another one at the community college?" K.O. asked.

LaVonne shook her head. "No, I walked across the street into A Good Yarn and decided I'd learn how to knit."

"That sounds good."

"Want to come, too?" LaVonne asked.

Every time her friend enrolled in a new course, she urged K.O. to take it with her. Because of finances and her job search, K.O. had always declined. This time, however, she felt she might be able to swing it. Not to mention the fact that she owed LaVonne . . . "I'll see."

"Really?" Even this little bit of enthusiasm seemed to delight LaVonne. "That's wonderful."

"I had a job interview on Wednesday," K.O. told her, squelching the desire to pin all her hopes on this one interview. Apple Blossom Books, the publisher Wynn had recommended, had called her in almost immediately. She'd met with the president and the marketing manager, and they'd promised to get back to her before Christmas. For the first time in a long while, K.O. felt optimistic. A publishing company, even a small one, would be ideal.

"And?" LaVonne prompted.

"And . . ." K.O. said, smiling. "I'm keeping my fingers crossed."

"That's just great! I know you've been looking for ages."

"The Christmas letters are going well, too," she added. "I wrote another one this week for a woman in Zach's office. She kept thinking she had time and then realized she didn't, so it was a rush job."

"You might really be on to something, you know. A little sideline business every Christmas."

"You aren't upset with me about what I did, are you?" K.O. asked, returning to her apology. "You've been such a good friend, and I wouldn't do anything in the world to hurt you."

"Nah," LaVonne assured her, petting Phillip, who'd jumped into her lap. "If anyone's to blame it's that horrible man. As far as I'm concerned, he's a fruitcake." That said, she took another bite of the slice she'd been enjoying.

Wynn had devised a rather complicated plan of escape. On Friday afternoon he would leave his office at three-thirty and pick K.O. up on the corner of Blossom Street and Port Avenue. Because he didn't want to risk going inside and being seen by his father, she'd agreed to wait on the curb with her overnight bag.

K.O. was packed and ready long before the time they'd arranged. At three, her phone rang. Without checking caller ID, she knew it had to be her sister.

"I can't believe Dr. Wynn Jeffries is actually coming to the house," she said and gave a shrill cry of excitement. "You can't *imagine* how jealous my friends are."

"No one's supposed to know about this," K.O. reminded her.

"No one knows exactly when he'll be here, but I did mention it to a few close friends."

"Zelda! You promised."

"I know, I know. I'm sorry, but I couldn't keep this to myself. You just don't understand what an honor it is to have Dr. Jeffries in my home."

"But . . ."

"Don't worry, no one knows it's this weekend," Zelda told her.

"You're *sure?*"

"I swear, all right?"

It would be a nightmare if a few dozen of Zelda's closest friends just happened to drop by the house unannounced. Unfortunately, K.O. didn't have any choice but to believe her.

"How are the girls?" K.O. asked, hoping the twins were up to their usual antics. She didn't want Zoe and Zara to be on their best behavior. That would ruin all her plans.

"They're fine. Well, mostly fine. Healthwise, they're both getting over ear infections."

Oh, dear. "You might've told me this before!" K.O. cried. Her mind shifted into overdrive. If the girls were sick, it would throw everything off. Wynn would insist their behavior was affected by how they were feeling.

"They've been on antibiotics for the last two weeks," Zelda said, breaking into her thoughts. "The doctor explained how important it is to finish the medicine, and they only have a couple of doses left. I wrote it all down for you and Dr. Jeffries, so there's no need to worry."

"Fine," K.O. said, relieved. "Anything else you're not telling me?"

Her sister went silent for a moment. "I can't think of anything. I've got a list of instructions for you and the phone numbers where we can be reached. I do appreciate this, you know."

K.O. in turn appreciated the opportunity to spend this time with the twins — and to share the experience with Wynn. At least they'd be able to stop tiptoeing around the subject of the Free Child movement.

"We have a Christmas tree," Zelda murmured as if she were admitting to a weakness of character. "Zach felt we needed one, and when I spoke to Dr. Jeffries last Monday he didn't discourage it. So I gave in, although I'm still not sure it's such a good idea."

"You made the right choice," K.O. told her.

"I hope so."

K.O. noticed the clock on her microwave

and was shocked to see that it was time to meet Wynn. "Oh, my goodness, I've got to go. I'll see you in about thirty minutes."

K.O. hung up the phone and hurried to put on her long wool coat, hat and scarf. Grabbing her purse and overnight bag, she rushed outside. Traffic was heavy, and it was already getting dark. She'd planned to be waiting at the curb so when Wynn pulled up, she could quickly hop inside his car. Then they'd be on their way, with no one the wiser.

No sooner had she stepped out of the building than she saw Max Jeffries walking toward her. His cheeks were ruddy, as if he'd been out for a long stroll.

"Well, hello there, Katherine," he said cheerfully. "How are you this fine cold day?"

"Ah . . ." She glanced furtively around. "I'm going to my sister's tonight," she said when he looked pointedly at her small suitcase.

"Wynn's away himself."

"Pure coincidence," she told him and realized how guilty she sounded.

Max chuckled. "Business trip, he said."

She nodded, moving slowly toward the nearby corner of Blossom and Port. She kept her gaze focused on the street, fearing she was about to give everything away.

"I'm healing well," Max told her conversationally. "I had a couple of rough days, but the pain is much better now."

"I'm glad to hear it."

"Yes, me, too. I never want to see that crazy cat woman again as long as I live."

It demanded restraint not to immediately defend her friend, but K.O. managed. "I see your memory's back," she said instead, all the while keeping a lookout for Wynn.

"Oh, yes, it returned within a day or two. In some ways," he sighed, "I wished it hadn't. Because now all I can think about is how that vicious feline latched on to my arm."

Not wanting to give Max an excuse to continue the conversation, K.O. threw him a vague smile.

"Have you ever seen so much blood in your life?" he said with remarkable enthusiasm.

"Uh, no," she murmured. Since it was her towels that had cleaned it up, she had to confess there'd been lots.

"My son seems to be quite taken with you," Max said next.

As badly as she wanted to urge Max to go about his business, K.O. couldn't ignore that particular comment. Not when Max dropped this little morsel at her feet —

much as Martin had presented her with the catnip mouse. "He does? Really?"

Max nodded.

"He talks about me?"

"Hmm. It's more a question of what he doesn't say than what he does. He was always an intense child. As a youngster . . . Well, I'm sure you don't have time to go into that right now."

K.O. thought she could see Wynn's car. "I don't . . . I'm sorry."

"Take my word for it, Wynn's interested in you."

K.O. felt like dancing in the street. "I'm interested in him, too," she admitted.

"Good, good," Max said expansively. "Well, I'd better get back inside. Have a nice weekend."

"I will. Thank you." It did look like Wynn's car. His timing was perfect — or almost. She hoped that when he reached the curb, his father would be inside the building.

Just then the front doors opened and out stepped LaVonne. She froze in midstep when she saw Wynn's father. He froze, too.

K.O. watched as LaVonne's eyes narrowed. She couldn't see Max's face, but from LaVonne's reaction, she assumed he shared her resentment. They seemed unwilling to walk past each other, and both stood there, looking wildly in all directions except ahead. If it hadn't been so sad, it would've been laughable.

K.O. could see that it was definitely Wynn's car. He smiled when he saw her and started to ease toward the curb. At the same moment, he noticed his father and LaVonne and instantly pulled back, merging into traffic again. He drove straight past K.O.

Now LaVonne and Max were staring at each other. They still hadn't moved, and people had to walk around them as they stood in the middle of the sidewalk.

K.O. had to find a way to escape without being detected. As best as she could figure, Wynn had to drive around the block. With one-way streets and heavy traffic, it might take him ten minutes to get back to Blossom. If she hurried, she might catch him on Port Avenue or another side street and avoid letting Max see them together.

"I think my ride's here," she said, backing away and dragging her suitcase with her.

They ignored her.

"Bye," she said, waving her hand.

This, too, went without comment. "I'll see you both later," she said, rushing past them and down the sidewalk.

Again there was no response.

K.O. didn't dare look back. Blossom

Street had never seemed so long. She rounded the corner and walked some distance down Port, waiting until she saw Wynn's car again. Raising her arm as if hailing a taxi, she managed to catch his attention.

Wynn pulled up to the curb, reached over and opened the passenger door. "That was a close call," he murmured as she climbed inside.

"You have no idea," she said, shaking her head.

"Is everything all right?" he asked.

"I don't know and, frankly, I don't want to stick around and find out."

Wynn chuckled. "I don't, either," he said, rejoining the stream of traffic.

They were off on what she hoped would be a grand adventure in the land of Z.

Chapter 15

"This is Zoe," K.O. said as her niece wrapped one arm around her leg. After a half-hour of instructions, Zelda was finally out the door, on her way to meet Zach at the hotel. The twins stood like miniature statues, dressed in jean coveralls and red polka-dot shirts, with their hair in pigtails. They each stared up at Wynn.

"No, I'm Zara."

K.O. narrowed her eyes, unsure whether to believe the child. The twins were identical and seemed to derive great satisfaction from fooling people, especially their parents.

"Zoe," K.O. challenged. "Tell the truth."

"I'm hungry."

"It'll be dinnertime soon," K.O. promised.

Zoe — and she felt sure it *was* Zoe — glared up at her. "I'm hungry *now*. I want to eat *now*." She punctuated her demand by stamping her foot. Her twin joined in, shouting that she, too, was hungry.

"I want dinner *now*," Zara insisted.

Wynn smiled knowingly. "Children shouldn't be forced to eat on a schedule. If they're hungry, we should feed them no matter what the clock says."

Until then, the girls had barely acknowledged Wynn. All of a sudden, he was their best friend. Both beamed brilliant smiles in his direction, then marched over and stood next to him, as though aligning themselves with his theories.

"What would you like for dinner?" he asked, squatting down so he was at eye level with them.

"Hot dogs," Zoe said, and Zara agreed. The two Yorkies, Zero and Zorro, seemed to approve, because they barked loudly and then scampered into the kitchen.

"I'll check the refrigerator," K.O. told him. Not long ago, Zelda hadn't allowed her daughters anywhere near hot dogs. She considered them unhealthy, low-quality fare that was full of nitrates and other preservatives. But nothing was off limits since Zelda had read *The Free Child* and become a convert.

"I'll help you look," Zara volunteered and tearing into the kitchen, threw open the refrigerator door and peered inside.

Not wanting to be left out, Zoe dragged

over a kitchen chair and climbed on top. She yanked open the freezer and started tossing frozen food onto the floor. Zero and Zorro scrambled to get out of the way of flying frozen peas and fish.

"There aren't any hot dogs," K.O. said after a few minutes. "Let's choose something else." After all, it was only four o'clock and she was afraid that if the girls ate too early, they'd be hungry again later in the evening.

"I *want* a hot dog," Zara shouted.

"Me, too," Zoe chimed in, as though eating wieners was a matter of eternal significance.

Wynn stood in the kitchen doorway. "I can run to the store."

K.O. couldn't believe her ears. She hated to see him cater to the whims of Zoe and Zara, but far be it from her to object. If he was willing to go to those lengths to get the twins the meal they wanted, she'd let him do it.

"Isn't that nice of Dr. Jeffries?" K.O. asked her nieces.

Both girls ignored her and Wynn.

K.O. followed him into the other room, where Wynn retrieved his jacket from the hall closet. "I'll be back soon," he said.

"I'll put together a salad and —"

"Let the girls decide if they want a salad," Wynn interrupted. "Given the option, children will choose a well-balanced diet on their own. We as adults shouldn't be making these decisions for them."

K.O. had broken down and bought a copy of *The Free Child* at a small bookstore that had recently opened on Blossom Street. She'd skimmed it last night, so she knew this advice was in the book, stated in exactly those words. She might not approve, but for tonight she was determined to follow his lead. So she kept her mouth shut. Not that it was easy.

While the girls were occupied, he planted a gentle kiss on her lips, smiled and then was out the door.

It was now three days since they'd been able to spend time together. With that one short kiss, a lovely warmth spread through her. She closed the door after him and was leaning against it when she noticed that the twins had turned to stare at her. "While we're waiting for Wynn to get back, would you like me to read you a story?" she asked. The salad discussion could wait.

The girls readily agreed, and the three of them settled on the sofa. She was only a few pages into the book when both Zoe and Zara slumped over, asleep. Before Zelda left, she'd said the twins had been awake since five that morning, excited about Katherine's visit. Apparently they no longer took naps. This was something else Wynn had advised. Children would sleep when they needed to, according to him. Regimented naptimes stifled children's ability to understand their internal clocks. Well, Zoe and Zara's clocks had obviously wound down — and K.O. was grateful.

The quiet was so blissful that she leaned her head back and rested her own eyes. The tranquility didn't last long, however. In less than fifteen minutes, Wynn was back from the store, carrying a plastic bag with wieners and fresh buns. The dogs barked frantically as he entered the house, waking both children.

"Here they are," he announced as if he brandished an Olympic gold medal.

Zara yawned. "I'm not hungry anymore."

"Me, neither," Zoe added.

It probably wasn't the most tactful thing to do, but K.O. smiled triumphantly.

"That's okay. We can wait until later," Wynn said, completely nonplussed.

He really was good with the girls and seemed to enjoy spending time with them. While K.O. set the kitchen table and cleared away the clutter that had accumulated everywhere, Wynn sat down and talked to the twins. The girls showed him the Christmas tree and the stockings that hung over the fireplace and the nativity scene set up on the formal dining room table.

K.O. heard Zoe mention her imaginary horse named Blackie. Not to be outdone, Zara declared that *her* imaginary horse was named Brownie. Wynn listened to them seriously and even scooted over to make room for the horses on the sofa. K.O. was grateful that Wynn was sharing responsibility for the girls, whose constant demands quickly drained her.

"I'm hungry now," Zoe informed them half an hour later.

"I'll start the hot dogs," K.O. said, ready for dinner herself.

"I want pancakes."

"With syrup," Zara said. Zoe nodded.

K.O. looked at Wynn, who shrugged as if it was no big deal.

"Then pancakes it is," K.O. agreed. She'd let him cope with the sugar high. For the next ten minutes she was busy mixing batter and frying the pancakes. The twins wanted chocolate syrup and strawberry jam on top, with bananas and granola. Actually, it didn't taste nearly as bad as K.O. had feared.

According to her sister's instructions, the girls were to be given their medication with meals. After dinner, Zoe and Zara climbed down from their chairs. When K.O. asked them to take their plates to the sink, they complied without an argument or even a complaint.

"Time for your medicine," K.O. told them next. She removed two small bottles filled with pink antibiotic from the refrigerator.

The two girls raced about the kitchen, shrieking, with the dogs yapping at their heels. They seemed incapable of standing still.

"Girls," K.O. ordered sternly. "Take your medicine and then you can run around." The way they were dashing back and forth, it was difficult to see who was who.

Zara skidded to a stop and dutifully opened her mouth. Carefully measuring out the liquid, K.O. filled the spoon and popped it into the child's mouth. Immediately afterward, the twins took off in a frenzied race around the kitchen table.

"Zoe," K.O. said, holding the second bottle and a clean spoon and waiting for the mayhem to die down so she could dispense the correct dose to her other niece. "Your turn."

The twin appeared in front of her, mouth

open. K.O. poured medicine onto the spoon. About to give it to Zoe, she hesitated. "You're not Zoe. You're Zara."

"I'm Zoe," she insisted. Although the girls were identical, K.O. could usually tell one from the other, partly by their personalities. Zara had the stronger, more dominant nature. "Are you sure?" she asked.

The little girl nodded vigorously. Uncertain, K.O. reluctantly gave her the medication. The twins continued to chase each other about the kitchen, weaving their way around and between Wynn and K.O. The dogs dashed after them, yapping madly.

Wynn asked, "Is everything all right?"

K.O. still held the empty spoon. "I have a horrible feeling I just gave two doses to the same girl."

"You can trust the twins to tell you the truth," Wynn pronounced. "Children instinctively know when it's important to tell the truth."

"Really?" K.O. couldn't help worrying.

"Of course. It's in the book," Wynn said as if quoting Scripture.

"You didn't feed Blackie and Brownie," Zara cried when K.O. tossed the leftover pancakes in the garbage.

"Then we must." Wynn proceeded to remove the cold pancakes and tear them

210

into small pieces. Zero and Zorro leaped off the ground in an effort to snatch up the leftovers. Zoe and Zara sat on the floor and fed the dogs and supposedly their imaginary pets, as well.

The yapping dogs were giving K.O. a headache. "How about if I turn on the television," she suggested, shouting to be heard above the racket made by the girls and the dogs.

The twins hollered their approval, but the show that flashed onto the screen was a Christmas cartoon featuring none other than Santa himself. Jolly old soul that he was, Santa laughed and loaded his sleigh while the girls watched with rapt attention. Knowing how her sister felt, K.O. figured this was probably the first time they'd seen Santa all season. K.O. glanced at Wynn, who was frowning back.

"Let's see what else is on," K.O. said quickly.

"I want to watch Santa," Zoe shouted.

"Me, too," Zara muttered.

Wynn sat on the sofa between them and wrapped his arms around their small shoulders. "This show is about a character called Santa Claus," he said in a solicitous voice.

Both girls were far too involved in the program to be easily distracted by adult conversation.

"Sometimes mommies and daddies like to make believe, and while they don't mean to lie, they can mislead their children," he went on.

Zoe briefly tore her gaze away from the television screen. "Like Santa, you mean?"

Wynn smiled. "Like Santa," he agreed.

"We know he's not real," Zoe informed them with all the wisdom of a five-year-old.

"Santa is really Mommy and Daddy," Zara explained. "*Everyone* knows that."

"They do?"

Both girls nodded.

Zoe's eyes turned serious. "We heard Mommy and Daddy fighting about Santa and we almost told them it doesn't matter 'cause we already know."

"We like getting gifts from him, though," Zara told them.

"Yeah, I like Santa," Zoe added.

"But he's not real," Wynn said, sounding perfectly logical.

"Mommy's real," Zara argued. "And Daddy, too."

"Yes, but . . ." Wynn seemed determined to argue further, but stopped when he happened to glance at K.O. He held her gaze a moment before looking away.

K.O. did her best to keep quiet, but apparently Wynn realized how difficult that was, because he clammed up fast enough.

The next time she looked at the twins, Zara had slumped over to one side, eyes drooping. K.O. gently shook the little girl's shoulders but Zara didn't respond. Still fearing she might have given one twin a double dose of the antibiotic, she knelt down in front of the other child.

"Zoe," she asked, struggling to keep the panic out of her voice. "Did you get your medicine or did Zara swallow both doses?"

Zoe grinned and pantomimed zipping her mouth closed.

"Zoe," K.O. said again. "This is important. We can't play games when medicine is involved." So much for Wynn's theory that children instinctively knew when it was necessary to tell the truth.

"Zara likes the taste better'n me."

"Did you take your medicine or did Zara take it for you?" Wynn asked.

Zoe smiled and shook her head, indicating that she wasn't telling.

Zara snored, punctuating the conversation.

"Did you or did you not take your medicine?" Wynn demanded, nearly yelling.

Tears welled in Zoe's eyes. She buried her

face in K.O.'s lap and refused to answer Wynn.

"This isn't a joke," he muttered, clearly losing his patience with the twins.

"Zoe," K.O. cautioned. "You heard Dr. Jeffries. It's important for us to know if you took your medication."

The little girl raised her head, then slowly nodded. "It tastes bad, but I swallowed it all down."

"Good." Relief flooded K.O. "Thank you for telling the truth."

"I don't like your friend," she said, sticking her tongue out at Wynn. "He yells."

"I only yelled because . . . you made me," Wynn countered. He marched to the far side of the room, and K.O. reflected that he didn't sound so calm and reasonable anymore.

"Why don't we all play a game?" she suggested.

Zara raised her head sleepily from the sofa edge. "Can we play Old Maid?" she asked, yawning.

"I want to play Candyland," Zoe mumbled.

"Why don't we play both?" K.O. said, and they did. In fact, they played for two hours straight, watched television and then drank hot chocolate.

"Shall we take a bath now?" K.O. asked, hoping that would tire the girls out enough to want to go to bed. She didn't know where they got their stamina, but her own was fading rapidly.

The twins were eager to do something altogether different and instantly raced out of the room.

Wynn looked like he could use a break — and he hadn't even seen them at their most challenging. All in all, the girls were exhibiting good behavior, or what passed for good in the regime of the Free Child.

"I'll run the bath water," K.O. told Wynn as he gathered up the cards and game pieces. Had she been on her own, K.O. would have insisted the twins pick up after themselves.

While the girls were occupied in their bedroom, she put on a Christmas CD she particularly liked and started the bath. When she glanced into the living room, she saw Wynn collapsed on the sofa, legs stretched out.

"It hasn't been so bad," he said, as though that was proof his theories were working well. "As soon as the twins are down, we can talk," he murmured, "about us . . ."

K.O. wasn't ready for that, feeling he should spend more time with the girls. She felt honor-bound to remind Wynn of what he'd written in his book. "Didn't you say that children know when they need sleep and we as adults should trust them to set their own schedules?"

He seemed about to argue with her, but then abruptly sat up and pointed across the room. "What's that?"

A naked dog strolled into the living room. Rather, a hairless dog.

"Zero? Zorro?" K.O. asked. "Oh, my goodness!" She dashed into the bathroom to discover Zara sitting on the floor with Wynn's electric shaver. A pile of brown-and-black dog hair littered the area.

"What happened?" Wynn cried, hard on her heels. His mouth fell open when he saw the girls intent on their task. They'd gone through his toiletries, which were spread across the countertop next to the sink. K.O. realized that the hum of the shaver had been concealed by the melodious strains of "Silent Night." "What are you doing?"

"We're giving haircuts," Zara announced. "Do you want one?"

CHAPTER 16

Two hours later, at ten-thirty, both Zoe and Zara were in their beds and asleep. This was no small accomplishment. After half a dozen stories, the girls were finally down for the night. K.O. tiptoed out of the room and as quietly as possible closed the door. Wynn was just ahead of her and looked as exhausted as she felt.

Zero regarded K.O. forlornly from the hallway. The poor dog had been almost completely shaved. He stared up at her, hairless and shivering. Zorro still had half his hair. The Yorkshire terrier's left side had been sheared before K.O. managed to snatch the razor out of her niece's hand. Last winter Zelda had knit tiny dog sweaters, which K.O. found, and with Wynn's help slipped over the two terriers. At least they'd be warm, although neither dog seemed especially grateful.

K.O. sank down on the sofa beside Wynn,

with the dogs nestled at their feet. Breathing out a long, deep sigh, she gazed up at the ceiling. Wynn was curiously quiet.

"I feel like going to bed myself," she murmured when she'd recovered enough energy to speak.

"What time are your sister and brother-in-law supposed to return?" Wynn asked with what seemed to require an extraordinary amount of effort.

"Zelda said they should be home by three."

"That late?"

K.O. couldn't keep the grin off her face. It was just as she'd hoped. She wouldn't have to argue about the problem with his Free Child theories, since he'd been able to witness for himself the havoc they caused.

Straightening, K.O. suggested they listen to some more music.

"That won't disturb them, will it?" he asked when she got up to put on another CD. Evidently he had no interest in anything that might wake the girls.

"I should hope not." She found the Christmas CD she'd given to Zelda two years earlier, and inserted it in the player. It featured a number of pop artists. Smiling over at Wynn, she lowered the volume. John Denver's voice reached softly into the room, singing "Joy to the World."

Wynn turned off the floor lamp, so the only illumination came from the Christmas-tree lights. The mood was cheerful and yet relaxed.

For the first time in days they were alone. The incident with Wynn's father and the demands of the twins were the last things on K.O.'s mind.

Wynn placed his arm across the back of the sofa and she sat close to him, resting her head against his shoulder. All they needed now was a glass of wine and a kiss or two. Romance swirled through the room with the music and Christmas lights. Wynn must've felt it, too, because he turned her in his arms. K.O. started to close her eyes, anticipating his kiss, when she caught a movement from the corner of her eye.

She gasped.

A mouse . . . a rodent ran across the floor.

Instantly alarmed, K.O. jerked away from Wynn.

He bolted upright. "What is it?"

"A mouse." She hated mice. "There," she cried, covering her mouth to stifle a scream. She pointed as the rodent scampered under the Christmas tree.

Wynn leaped to his feet. "I see it."

Apparently so did Zero, because he let out

a yelp and headed right for the tree. Zorro followed.

K.O. brought both feet onto the sofa and hugged her knees. It was completely unreasonable — and so clichéd — to be terrified of a little mouse. But she was. While logic told her a mouse was harmless, that knowledge didn't help.

"You have to get it out of here," she whimpered as panic set in.

"I'll catch it," he shouted and dived under the Christmas tree, toppling it. The tree slammed against the floor, shattering several bulbs. Ornaments rolled in all directions. The dogs ran for cover. Fortunately the tree was still plugged in because it offered what little light was available.

Unable to watch, K.O. hid her eyes. She wondered what Wynn would do if he did manage to corner the rodent. The thought of him killing it right there in her sister's living room was intolerable.

"Don't kill it," she insisted and removed her hands from her eyes to find Wynn on his hands and knees, staring at her.

The mouse darted across the floor and raced under the sofa, where K.O. just happened to be sitting.

Zero and Zorro ran after it, yelping frantically.

K.O. screeched and scrambled to a standing position on the sofa. Not knowing what else to do, she bounced from one cushion to the other.

Zero had buried his nose as far as it would go under the sofa. Zorro dashed back and forth on the carpet. As hard as she tried, K.O. couldn't keep still and began hopping up and down, crying out in abject terror. She didn't care if she woke the girls or not, there was a mouse directly beneath her feet . . . somewhere. For all she knew, it could have crawled into the sofa itself.

That thought made her jump from the middle of the sofa, over the armrest and onto the floor, narrowly missing Zero. The lamp fell when she landed, but she was able to catch it seconds before it crashed to the floor. As she righted the lamp, she flipped it on, providing a welcome circle of light.

Meanwhile, Barry Manilow crooned out "The Twelve Days of Christmas."

Still on all fours, Wynn crept across the carpet to the sofa, which he overturned. As it pitched onto its back, the mouse shot out.

Directly at K.O.

She screamed.

Zero yelped.

Zorro tore fearlessly after it.

K.O. screamed again and grabbed a basket

in which Zelda kept her knitting. She emptied the basket and, more by instinct than anything else, flung it over the mouse, trapping him.

Wynn sat up with a shocked look. "You got him!"

Both dogs stood guard by the basket, sniffing at the edges. Zero scratched the carpet.

Zelda's yarn and needles were a tangled mess on the floor but seemed intact. Breathless, K.O. stared at the basket, not knowing what to do next. "It had a brown tail," she commented.

Wynn nodded. "I noticed that, too."

"I've never seen a mouse with a brown tail before."

"It's an African brown-tailed mouse," he said, sounding knowledgeable. "I saw a documentary on them."

"African mice are here in the States?" She wondered if Animal Control knew about this.

He nodded again. "So I gather."

"What do we do now?" Because Wynn seemed to know more about this sort of thing, she looked to him for the answer.

"Kill it," he said without a qualm.

Zero and Zorro obviously agreed, because they both growled and clawed at the carpet, asking for the opportunity to do it themselves.

"No way!" K.O. objected. She couldn't allow him to kill it. The terriers, either. Although mice terrified her, K.O. couldn't bear to hurt any of God's creatures. "All I want you to do is get that brown-tailed mouse out of here." As soon as Zelda returned, K.O. planned to suggest she call a pest control company to inspect the entire house. Although, if there were other mice around, she didn't want to know it. . . .

"All right," Wynn muttered. "I'll take it outside and release it."

He got a newspaper and knelt down next to the dogs. Carefully, inch by inch, he slid the paper beneath the upended basket. When he'd finished that, he stood and carried the whole thing to the front door. Zero and Zorro followed, leaping up on their hind legs and barking wildly.

K.O. hurried to open first the door and then the screen. The cold air felt good against her heated face.

Wynn stepped onto the porch while K.O. held back the dogs by closing the screen door. They both objected strenuously and braced their front paws against the door, watching Wynn's every movement.

K.O. turned her back as Wynn released

the African brown-tailed mouse into the great unknown. She wished the critter a pleasant life outside.

"Is it gone?" she asked when Wynn came back into the house, careful to keep Zero and Zorro from escaping and racing after the varmint.

"It's gone, and I didn't even need to touch it," he assured her. He closed the door.

K.O. smiled up at him. "My hero," she whispered.

Wynn playfully flexed his muscles. "Anything else I can do for you, my fair damsel?"

Looping her arms around his neck, K.O. backed him up against the front door and rewarded him with a warm, moist kiss. Wynn wrapped his arms about her waist and half lifted her from the carpet.

"You *are* my hero," she whispered between kisses. "You saved me from that killer mouse."

"The African brown-tailed killer rat."

"It was a *rat?*"

"A small one," he murmured, and kissed her again before she could ask more questions.

"A baby rat?" That meant there must be parents around and possibly siblings, perhaps any number of other little rats. "What makes you think it was a rat?" she demanded, fast losing interest in kissing.

"He was fat. But perhaps he was just a fat mouse."

"Ah . . ."

"You're still grateful?"

"Very grateful, but —"

He kissed her again, then abruptly broke off the kiss. His eyes seemed to focus on something across the room.

K.O. tensed, afraid he'd seen another mouse. Or rat. Or rodent of some description.

It took genuine courage to glance over her shoulder, but she did it anyway. Fortunately she didn't see anything — other than an overturned Christmas tree, scattered furniture and general chaos brought about by the Great Brown-Tailed Mouse Hunt.

"The fishbowl has blue water," he said.

"Blue water?" K.O. dropped her arms and stared at the counter between the kitchen and the living room, where the fishbowl sat. Sure enough, the water was a deep blue.

Wynn walked across the room.

Before K.O. could ask what he was doing, Wynn pushed up his sweater sleeve and thrust his hand into the water. "Just as I thought," he muttered, retrieving a gold pen.

After she'd found the twins with Wynn's electric shaver, she realized, they'd opened his overnight case.

"This is a gold fountain pen," he told her, holding up the dripping pen. "As it happens, this is a *valuable* gold fountain pen."

"With blue ink," K.O. added. She didn't think it could be too valuable, since it was leaking.

She picked up the bowl with both hands and carried it into the kitchen, setting it in the sink. Scooping out the two goldfish, she put them in a temporary home — a coffee cup full of fresh, clean water — and refilled the bowl.

Wynn was pacing the kitchen floor behind her.

"Does your book say anything about situations like this?" she couldn't resist asking.

He glared at her and apparently that was all the answer he intended to give.

"Aunt Katherine?" one of the twins shouted. "Come quick." K.O. heard unmistakable panic in the little girl's voice.

Soon the two girls were both crying out.

Hurrying into the bedroom with Wynn right behind her, K.O. found Zoe and Zara weeping loudly.

"What's wrong?" she asked.

"Freddy's gone," Zoe wailed.

"Freddy?" she repeated. "Who's Freddy?"

"Our hamster," Zoe explained, pointing at

what K.O. now recognized as a cage against the far wall. "He must've figured out how to open his cage."

A chill went through her. "Does Freddy have a brown tail and happen to be a little chubby?" she asked the girls.

Hope filled their eyes as they nodded eagerly.

K.O. scowled at Wynn. African browntailed mouse, indeed.

CHAPTER 17

Thankfully, Wynn rescued poor Freddy, who was discovered shivering in a corner of the porch. The girls were relieved to have their hamster back, and neither mentioned the close call Freddy had encountered with certain death. After calming the twins, it took K.O. and Wynn an hour to clean up the living room. By then, they were both cranky and tired.

Saturday morning, Zoe and Zara decided on wieners for breakfast. Knowing Wynn would approve, K.O. cooked the hot dogs he'd purchased the night before. However, the unaccustomed meat didn't settle well in Zoe's tummy and she threw up on her breakfast plate. Zara insisted that all she wanted was orange juice poured over dry cereal. So that was what she got.

For the rest of the morning, Wynn remained pensive and remote. He helped her with the children but didn't want to talk. In fact, he seemed more than eager to get back to Blossom Street. When Zelda and Zach showed up that afternoon, he couldn't quite hide his relief. The twins hugged K.O. good-bye and Wynn, too.

While Wynn loaded the car, K.O. talked to Zelda about holiday plans. Zelda asked her to join the family for Christmas Eve dinner and church, but not Christmas Day, which they'd be spending with Zach's parents. K.O. didn't mind. She'd invite LaVonne to dinner at her place. Maybe she'd include Wynn and his father, too, despite the disastrous conclusion of the last social event she'd hosted for this same group. Still, when she had the chance, she'd discuss it with Wynn.

On the drive home, Wynn seemed especially quiet.

"The girls are a handful, aren't they?" she asked, hoping to start a conversation.

He nodded.

She smiled to herself, remembering Wynn's expression when Zoe announced that their hamster had escaped. Despite his reproachful silence, she laughed. "I promise not to mention that rare African brown-tailed mouse again, but I have to tell LaVonne."

"I never said it was rare."

"Oh, sorry, I thought you had." One look told her Wynn wasn't amused. "Come on, Wynn," she said, as they merged with the freeway traffic. "You have to admit it was a little ridiculous."

He didn't appear to be in the mood to admit anything. "Are you happy?" he asked.

"What do you mean?"

"You proved your point, didn't you?"

So that was the problem. "If you're referring to how the girls behaved then, yes, I suppose I did."

"You claimed that after your sister read my book, they changed into undisciplined hellions."

"Well . . ." Wasn't it obvious? "They're twins," she said, trying to sound conciliatory, "and as such they've always needed a lot of attention. Some of what happened on Friday evening might have happened without the influence of your child-rearing theories. Freddy would've escaped whether Zelda read your book or not."

"Very funny."

"I wasn't trying to be funny. Frankly, rushing to the store to buy hot dogs because that's what the girls wanted for dinner is over the top, in my opinion. I feel it teaches them to expect that their every whim must be met."

"I beg to differ. My getting the dinner they wanted showed them that I cared about their likes and dislikes."

"Two hours of sitting on the floor playing Old Maid said the same thing," she inserted.

"I let you put them to bed even though they clearly weren't ready for sleep."

"I beg to differ," she said, a bit more forcefully than she'd intended. "Zoe and Zara were both yawning when they came out of the bath. I asked them if they wanted to go to bed."

"What you asked," he said stiffly, "was if they were *ready* for bed."

"And the difference is?"

"Two hours of storytime while they wore us both out."

"What would you have done?" she asked.

His gaze didn't waver from the road. "I would've allowed them to play quietly in their room until they'd tired themselves out."

Quietly? He had to be joking. Wynn seemed to have conveniently forgotten that during the short time they were on their own, Zoe and Zara had gotten into his overnight bag. Thanks to their creative use of his personal things, the goldfish now had a bluish tint. The two Yorkies were nearly hairless. She could argue that because the girls considered themselves *free,* they didn't see anything wrong with opening his bag. The lack of boundaries created confusion and misunderstanding.

"Twins are not the norm," he challenged. "They encourage ill behavior in each other."

"However, before Zelda read your book, they were reasonably well-behaved children."

"Is that a fact?" He sounded as though he didn't believe her.

"Yes," she said swiftly. "Zoe and Zara were happy and respectful and kind. Some would even go so far as to say they were well-adjusted. Now they constantly demand their own way. They're unreasonable, selfish and difficult." She was only getting started and dragged in another breath. "Furthermore, it used to be a joy to spend time with them and now it's a chore. And if you must know, I blame you and that blasted book of yours." There, she'd said it.

A stark silence followed.

"You don't mince words, do you?"

"No . . ."

"I respect that. I wholeheartedly disagree, but I respect your right to state your opinion."

The tension in the car had just increased by about a thousand degrees.

"After this weekend, you still disagree?" She was astonished he'd actually said that, but then she supposed his ego was on the line.

"I'm not interested in arguing with you, Katherine."

She didn't want to argue with him, either. Still, she'd hoped the twins would convince him that while his theories might look good on paper, in reality they didn't work.

After Wynn exited the freeway, it was only a few short blocks to Blossom Street and the parking garage beneath their building. Wynn pulled into his assigned slot and turned off the engine.

Neither moved.

K.O. feared that the minute she opened the car door, it would be over, and she didn't want their relationship to end, not like this. Not now, with Christmas only nine days away.

She tried again. "I know we don't see eye to eye on everything —"

"No, we don't," he interrupted. "In many cases, it doesn't matter, but when it comes to my work, my livelihood, it does. Not only do you not accept my theories, you think they're ludicrous."

She opened her mouth to defend herself, then realized he was right. That was exactly what she thought.

"You've seen evidence that appears to contradict them and, therefore, you discount the years of research I've done in my field. The fact is, you don't respect my work."

Feeling wretched, she hung her head.

"I expected there to be areas in which we disagree, Katherine, but this is more than I can deal with. I'm sorry, but I think it would be best if we didn't see each other again."

If that was truly how he felt, then there was nothing left to say.

"I appreciate that you've been honest with me," he continued. "I'm sorry, Katherine — I know we both would've liked this to work, but we have too many differences."

She made an effort to smile. If she thought arguing with him would do any good, she would have. But the hard set of his jaw told her no amount of reasoning would reach him now. "Thank you for everything. Really, I mean that. You've made this Christmas the best."

He gave her a sad smile.

"Would it be all right — would you mind if I gave you a hug?" she asked. "To say goodbye?"

He stared at her for the longest moment, then slowly shook his head. "That wouldn't be a good idea," he whispered, opening the car door.

By the time K.O. was out of the vehicle, he'd already retrieved her overnight bag from the trunk.

She waited, but it soon became apparent that he had no intention of taking the elevator with her. It seemed he'd had about as much of her company as he could stand.

She stepped into the elevator with her bag and turned around. Before the doors closed, she saw Wynn leaning against the side of his car with his head down, looking dejected. K.O. understood the feeling.

It had been such a promising relationship. She'd never felt this drawn to a man, this attracted. If only she'd been able to keep her mouth shut — but, oh, no, not her. She'd wanted to prove her point, show him the error of his ways. She still believed he was wrong — well, mostly wrong — but now she felt petty and mean.

When the elevator stopped at the first floor, the doors slid open and K.O. got out. The first thing she did was collect her mail and her newspapers. She eyed the elevator, wondering if she'd ever see Wynn again, other than merely in passing, which would be painfully unavoidable.

After unpacking her overnight case and sorting through the mail, none of which interested her, she walked across the hall, hoping to talk to LaVonne.

Even after several long rings, LaVonne didn't answer her door. Perhaps she was doing errands.

Just as K.O. was about to walk away, her neighbor opened the door just a crack and peered out.

"LaVonne, it's me."

"Oh, hi," she said.

"Can I come in?" K.O. asked, wondering why LaVonne didn't immediately invite her inside. She'd never hesitated to ask her in before.

"Ah . . . now isn't really a good time."

"Oh." That was puzzling.

"How about tomorrow?" LaVonne suggested.

"Sure." K.O. nodded. "Is Tom back?" she asked.

"Tom?"

"Your cat."

"Oh, oh . . . that Tom. Yes, he came home this morning."

K.O. was pleased to hear that. She dredged up a smile. "I'll talk to you tomorrow, then."

"Yes," she agreed. "Tomorrow."

K.O. started across the hall, then abruptly turned back. "You might care to know that the Raisin Bran got it all wrong."

"I beg your pardon?" LaVonne asked, narrowing her gaze.

"I think you might've read the kitty litter wrong, too. But then again, that particular box accurately describes my love life."

LaVonne opened the door a fraction of an inch wider. "Do you mean to tell me you're no longer seeing Wynn?"

K.O. nodded. "Apparently we were both wrong in thinking Wynn was the man for me."

"He is," LaVonne said confidently.

K.O. sighed. "I wish he was. I genuinely like Wynn. When I first discovered he was the author of that loony book my sister read . . ." Realizing what she'd just said, K.O. began again. "When I discovered he wrote the book she'd read, I had my doubts."

"It *is* a loony book," LaVonne said.

"I should never have told him how I felt."

"You were honest."

"Yes, but I was rude and hurtful, too." She shook her head mournfully. "We disagree on just about every aspect of child-rearing. He doesn't want to see me again and I don't blame him."

LaVonne stared at her for an intense moment. "You're falling in love with him."

"No, I'm not," she said, hoping to make

light of her feelings, but her neighbor was right. K.O. had known it the minute Wynn dived under the Christmas tree to save her from the not-so-rare African brown-tailed mouse. The minute he'd waved down the horse-drawn carriage and covered her knees with a lap robe and slipped his arm around her shoulders.

"Don't try to deny it," LaVonne said. "I don't really know what I saw in that Raisin Bran. Probably just raisins. But all along I've felt that Wynn's the man for you."

"I wish that was true," she said as she turned to go home. "But it's not."

As she opened her own door, she heard LaVonne talking. When she glanced back, she could hear her in a heated conversation with someone inside the condo. Unfortunately LaVonne was blocking the doorway, so K.O. couldn't see who it was.

"LaVonne?"

The door opened wider and out stepped Max Jeffries. "Hello, Katherine," he greeted her, grinning from ear to ear.

K.O. looked at her neighbor and then at Wynn's father. The last she'd heard, Max was planning to sue LaVonne for everything she had. Somehow, in the past twenty-four hours, he'd changed his mind.

"Max?" she said in an incredulous voice.

He grinned boyishly and placed his arm around LaVonne's shoulders.

"You see," LaVonne said, blushing a fetching shade of red. "My psychic talents might be limited, but you're more talented than you knew."

CHAPTER 18

K.O. was depressed. Even the fact that she'd been hired by Apple Blossom Books as their new publicist hadn't been enough to raise her spirits. She was scheduled to start work the day after New Year's and should've been thrilled. She was, only . . . nothing felt right without Wynn.

It was Christmas Eve and it should have been one of the happiest days of the year, but she felt like staying in bed. Her sister and family were expecting her later that afternoon, so K.O. knew she couldn't mope around the condo all day. She had things to do, food to buy, gifts to wrap, and she'd better get moving.

Putting on her coat and gloves, she walked out of her condo wearing a smile. She refused to let anyone know she was suffering from a broken heart.

"Katherine," LaVonne called the instant she saw her. She stood at the lobby mailbox as if she'd been there for hours, just waiting for K.O. "Merry Christmas!"

"Merry Christmas," K.O. returned a little too brightly. She managed a smile and with her shoulders squared, made her way to the door.

"Do you have any plans for Christmas?" her neighbor called after her.

K.O.'s mouth hurt from holding that smile for so long. She nodded. "I'm joining Zelda, Zach and the girls this evening, and then I thought I'd spend a quiet Christmas by myself." Needless to say, she hadn't issued any invitations, and she'd hardly seen LaVonne in days. Tomorrow she'd cook for herself. While doing errands this morning, she planned to purchase a small — very small — turkey. She refused to mope and feel lonely, not on Christmas Day.

"Have dinner with me," LaVonne said. "It'll just be me and the boys."

When K.O. hesitated, she added, "Tom, Phillip and Martin would love to see you. I'm cooking a turkey and all the fixings, and I'd be grateful for the company."

"Are you sure?"

"Of course I'm sure!"

K.O. didn't take long to consider her friend's invitation. "I'd love to, then. What would you like me to bring?"

"Dessert," LaVonne said promptly. "Something yummy and special for Christmas."

"All right." They agreed on a time and K.O. left, feeling better than she had in days. Just as she was about to step outside, she turned back.

"How's Max?" she asked, knowing her neighbor was on good terms with Wynn's father. Exactly how good those terms were remained to be seen. She wondered fleetingly what the Jeffrieses were doing for Christmas, then decided it was none of her business. Still, the afternoon K.O. had found Max in LaVonne's condo, she'd been shocked to say the least. Their brief conversation the following day hadn't been too enlightening but maybe over Christmas dinner LaVonne would tell her what had happened — and what was happening now.

Flustered, LaVonne lowered her eyes as she sorted through a stack of mail that seemed to be mostly Christmas cards. "He's completely recovered. And," she whispered, "he's apologized to Tom."

A sense of pleasure shot through K.O. at this . . . and at the way LaVonne blushed. Apparently this was one romance that held promise. Her own had fizzled out fast enough. She'd come to truly like Wynn.

More than like . . . At the thought of him, an aching sensation pressed down on her. In retrospect, she wished she'd handled the situation differently. Because she couldn't resist, she had to ask, "Have you seen Wynn?"

Her friend nodded but the look in LaVonne's eyes told K.O. everything she dreaded.

"He's still angry, isn't he?"

LaVonne gave her a sad smile. "I'm sure everything will work out. I know what I saw in that Raisin Bran." She attempted a laugh.

"When you see him again, tell him . . ." She paused. "Tell him," she started again, then gave up. Wynn had made his feelings clear. He'd told her it would be best if they didn't see each other again, and he'd meant it. Nine days with no word told her he wasn't changing his mind. Well, she had her pride, too.

"What would you like me to tell him?" LaVonne asked.

"Nothing. It's not important."

"You could write him a letter," LaVonne suggested.

"Perhaps I will," K.O. said on her way out the door, but she knew she wouldn't. It was over.

Blossom Street seemed more alive than at

any other time she could remember. A group of carolers performed at the corner, songbooks in their hands. An elderly gentleman rang a bell for charity outside the French Café, which was crowded with customers. Seeing how busy the place was, K.O. decided to purchase her Christmas dessert now, before they completely sold out.

After adding a donation to the pot as she entered the café, she stood in a long line. When her turn finally came to order, she saw that one of the bakers was helping at the counter. K.O. knew Alix Townsend or, at least, she'd talked to her often enough to know her by name.

"Merry Christmas, K.O.," Alix said.

"Merry Christmas to you, too." K.O. surveyed the sweet delicacies behind the glass counter. "I need something that says Christmas," she murmured. The decorated cookies were festive but didn't seem quite right. A pumpkin pie would work, but it wasn't really special.

"How about a small Bûche de Noël," Alix said. "It's a traditional French dessert — a fancy cake decorated with mocha cream frosting and shaped to look like a Yule log. I baked it myself from a special recipe of the owner's."

"Bûche de Noël," K.O. repeated. It sounded perfect.

"They're going fast," Alix pointed out.

"Sold," K.O. said as the young woman went to collect one from the refrigerated case. It was then that K.O. noticed Alix's engagement ring.

"Will there be anything else?" Alix asked, setting the pink box on the counter and tying it with string.

"That diamond's new, isn't it?"

Grinning, Alix examined her ring finger. "I got it last week. Jordan couldn't wait to give it to me."

"Congratulations," K.O. told her. "When's the wedding?"

Alix looked down at the diamond as if she could hardly take her eyes off it. "June."

"That's fabulous."

"I'm already talking to Susannah Nelson — she owns the flower shop across the street. Jacqueline, my friend, insists we hold the reception at the Country Club. If it was up to me, Jordan and I would just elope, but his family would never stand for that." She shrugged in a resigned way. "I love Jordan, and I don't care what I have to do, as long as I get to be his wife."

The words echoed in K.O.'s heart as she walked out of the French Café with a final

"Merry Christmas." She didn't know Alix Townsend all that well, but she liked her. Alix was entirely without pretense. No one need doubt how she felt about any particular subject; she spoke her mind in a straightforward manner that left nothing to speculation.

K.O. passed Susannah's Garden, the flower shop, on her way to the bank. The owner and her husband stood out front, wishing everyone a Merry Christmas. As K.O. walked past, Susannah handed her a sprig of holly with bright red berries.

"Thank you — this is so nice," K.O. said, tucking the holly in her coat pocket. She loved the flower shop and the beauty it brought to the street.

"I want to let the neighborhood know how much I appreciate the support. I've only been in business since September and everyone's been so helpful."

"Here, have a cup of hot cider." Susannah's husband was handing out plastic cups from a small table set up beside him. "I'm Joe," he said.

"Hello, Joe. I'm Katherine O'Connor."

Susannah slid one arm around her husband's waist and gazed up at him with such adoration it was painful for K.O. to watch. Everywhere she turned, people were happy and in love. A knot formed in her throat. Putting on a happy, carefree face was getting harder by the minute.

Just then the door to A Good Yarn opened and out came Lydia Goetz and a man K.O. assumed must be her husband. They were accompanied by a young boy, obviously their son. Lydia paused when she saw K.O.

Lydia was well-known on the street.

"Were you planning to stop in here?" she asked, and cast a quick glance at her husband. "Brad convinced me to close early today. I already sent my sister home, but if you need yarn, I'd be happy to get it for you. In fact, you could even pay me later." She looked at her husband again, as if to make sure he didn't object to the delay. "It wouldn't take more than a few minutes. I know what it's like to run out of yarn when you only need one ball to finish a project."

"No, no, that's fine," K.O. said. She'd always wanted to learn to knit and now that LaVonne was taking a class, maybe she'd join, too.

"Merry Christmas!" Lydia tucked her arm in her husband's.

"Merry Christmas," K.O. returned. Soon they hurried down the street, with the boy trotting ahead.

Transfixed, K.O. stood there unmoving.

The lump that had formed in her throat grew huge. The whole world was in love, and she'd let the opportunity of her life slip away. She'd let Wynn go with barely a token protest, and that was wrong. If she believed in their love, she needed to fight for it, instead of pretending everything was fine without him. Because it wasn't. In fact, she was downright miserable, and it was time she admitted it.

She knew what she had to do. Afraid that if she didn't act quickly, she'd lose her nerve, K.O. ran back across the street and into her own building. Marching to the elevator, she punched the button and waited.

She wasn't even sure what she'd tell Wynn; she'd figure that out when she saw him. But seeing him was a necessity. She couldn't spend another minute like this. She'd made a terrible mistake, and so had he. If there was any chance of salvaging this relationship, she had to try.

Her heart seemed to be pounding at twice its normal rate as she rode the elevator up to Wynn's penthouse condominium. She'd only been inside once, and then briefly.

By the time she reached his front door, she was so dizzy she'd become light-headed. That didn't deter her from ringing the buzzer and waiting for what felt like an eternity.

Only it wasn't Wynn who opened the door. It was Max.

"Katherine," he said, obviously surprised to find her at his son's door. "Come in."

"Is Wynn available?" she asked, as winded as if she'd climbed the stairs instead of taking the elevator. Talking to Wynn — *now* — had assumed a sense of urgency.

Wynn stepped into the foyer and frowned when he saw her. "Katherine?" She could see the question in his eyes.

"Merry Christmas," Max said. He didn't seem inclined to leave.

"Could we talk?" she asked. "Privately?" She was terrified he'd tell her that everything had already been said, so she rushed to add, "Really, this will only take a moment and then I'll leave."

Wynn glanced at his father, who took the hint and reluctantly left the entryway.

K.O. remained standing there, clutching her purse with one hand and the pink box with the other. "I was out at the French Café and I talked to Alix."

"Alix?"

"She's one of the bakers and a friend of Lydia's — and Lydia's the lady who owns A Good Yarn. But that's not important.

What *is* important is that Alix received an engagement ring for Christmas. She's so happy and in love, and Lydia is, too, and Susannah from the flower shop and just about everyone on the street. It's so full of Christmas out there, and all at once it came to me that . . . that I couldn't let this Christmas pass with things between us the way they are." She stopped to take a deep breath.

"Katherine, I —"

"Please let me finish, otherwise I don't know if I'll have the courage to continue."

He motioned for her to speak.

"I'm so sorry, Wynn, for everything. For wanting to be right and then subjecting you to Zoe and Zara. Their behavior *did* change after Zelda read your book and while I can't say I agree with everything you —"

"This is an apology?" he asked, raising his eyebrows.

"I'm trying. I'm sincerely trying. Please hear me out."

He crossed his arms and looked away. In fact, he seemed to find something behind her utterly fascinating.

This wasn't the time to lose her courage. She went on, speaking quickly, so quickly that the words practically ran together. "Basically, I wanted to tell you it was rude of me to assume I knew more than you on the subject of children. It was presumptuous and self-righteous. I was trying to prove how wrong you were . . . are, and that I was right. To be honest, I don't know what's right or wrong. All I know is how much I miss you and how much it hurts that you're out of my life."

"I'm the one who's been presumptuous and self-righteous," Wynn said. "You *are* right, Katherine, about almost everything. It hasn't been easy for me to accept that, let alone face it."

"Oh, for heaven's sake, aren't you two going to kiss and make up?" Max demanded, coming back into the foyer. Apparently he'd been standing in the living room, out of sight, and had listened in on every word. "Wynn, if you let this woman walk away, then you're a fool. An even bigger fool than you know."

"I — I . . ." Wynn stuttered.

"You've been in love with her for weeks." Max shook his head as if this was more than obvious.

Wynn pinned his father with a fierce glare.

"You love me?" K.O. asked, her voice rising to a squeak. "Because I'm in love with you, too."

A light flickered in his eyes at her confession. "Katherine, I appreciate your coming. However, this is serious and it's something we both need to think over. It's too important — we can't allow ourselves to get caught up in emotions that are part of the holidays. We'll talk after Christmas, all right?"

"I can't do that," she cried.

"Good for you," Max shouted, encouraging her. "I'm going to phone LaVonne. This calls for champagne."

"What does?" Wynn asked.

"Us," she explained. "You and me. I love you, Wynn, and I can't bear the thought that I won't see you again. It's tearing me up. I don't *need* time to think about us. I already know how I feel, and if what your father says is true, you know how you feel about me."

"Well, I do need to think," he insisted. "I haven't figured out what I'm going to do yet, because I can't continue promoting a book whose theories I can no longer wholly support. Let me deal with that first."

"No," she said. "Love should come first." She stared into his eyes. "Love changes everything, Wynn." Then, because it was impossible to hold back for another second, she put down her purse and the Yule log and threw her arms around him.

252

Wynn was stiff and unbending, and then his arms circled her, too. "Are you always this stubborn?" he asked.

"Yes. Sometimes even more than this. Ask Zelda."

Wynn kissed her. His arms tightened around her, as if he found it hard to believe she was actually there in his embrace.

"That's the way to handle it," Max said from somewhere behind them.

Wynn and K.O. ignored him.

"He's been a real pain these last few days," Max went on. "But this should improve matters."

Wynn broke off the kiss and held her gaze. "We'll probably never agree on everything."

"Probably."

"I can be just as stubborn as you."

"That's questionable," she said with a laugh.

His lips found hers again, as if he couldn't bear not to kiss her. Each kiss required a bit more time and became a bit more involved.

"I don't believe in long courtships," he murmured, his eyes still closed.

"I don't, either," she said. "And I'm going to want children."

He hesitated.

"We don't need all the answers right this minute, do we, Dr. Jeffries?"

"About Santa —"

She interrupted him, cutting off any argument by kissing him. What resistance there was didn't last.

"I was about to suggest we could bring Santa out from beneath that sleigh," he whispered, his eyes briefly fluttering open.

"Really?" This was more than she'd dared hope.

"Really."

She'd been more than willing to forgo Santa as long as she had Wynn. But Santa *and* Wynn was better yet.

"No hamsters, though," he said firmly.

"Named Freddy," she added.

Wynn chuckled. "Or anything else."

The doorbell chimed and Max hurried to answer it, ushering LaVonne inside. The instant she saw Wynn and K.O. in each other's arms, she clapped with delight. "Didn't I tell you everything would work out?" she asked Max.

"You did, indeed."

LaVonne nodded sagely. "I think I may have psychic powers, after all. I saw it all plain as day in the leaves of my poinsettia," she proclaimed. "Just before Max called, two of them fell to the ground — together."

Despite herself, K.O. laughed. Until a few minutes ago, her love life had virtually disappeared. Now there was hope, real hope for her and Wynn to learn from each other and as LaVonne's prophecy — real or imagined — implied, grow together instead of apart.

"Champagne, anyone?" Max asked, bringing out a bottle.

Wynn still held K.O. and she wasn't objecting. "I need to hire you," he whispered close to her ear.

"Hire me?"

"I'm kind of late with my Christmas letter this year and I wondered if I could convince you to write one for me."

"Of course. It's on the house." With his arms around her waist, she leaned back and looked up at him. "Is there anything in particular you'd like me to say?"

"Oh, yes. You can write about the success of my first published book — and explain that there'll be a retraction in the next edition." He winked. "Or, if you prefer, you could call it a compromise."

K.O. smiled.

"And then I want you to tell my family and friends that I'm working on a new book that'll be called *The Happy Child,* and it'll be about creating appropriate boundaries within the Free Child system of parenting."

K.O. rewarded him with a lengthy kiss that

left her knees weak. Fortunately, he had a firm hold on her, and she on him.

"You can also mention the fact that there's going to be a wedding in the family."

"Two weddings," Max inserted as he handed LaVonne a champagne glass.

"Two?" LaVonne echoed shyly.

Max nodded, filling three more glasses. "Wynn and K.O.'s isn't the only romance that started out rocky. The way I figure it, if I can win Tom over, his mistress shouldn't be far behind."

"Oh, Max!"

"Is there anything else you'd like me to say in your Christmas letter?" K.O. asked Wynn.

"Oh, yes, there's plenty more, but I think we'll leave it for the next Christmas letter and then the one after that." He brought K.O. close once more and hugged her tight.

She loved being in his arms — and in his life. Next year's Christmas letter would be from both of them. It would be all about how happy they were . . . and every word would be true.

ABOUT THE AUTHOR

Debbie Macomber, the author of *6 Rainier Drive, Susannah's Garden, 50 Harbor Street, A Good Yarn* and *The Shop on Blossom Street,* has become a leading voice in women's fiction worldwide. Her work has appeared on every major bestseller list, including those of the *New York Times, USA TODAY* and *Publishers Weekly.* She is a multiple award winner, and won the 2005 Quill Award for Best Romance. There are more than sixty million copies of her books in print.

We hope you have enjoyed this Large Print book. Other Thorndike, Wheeler, and Chivers Press Large Print books are available at your library or directly from the publishers.

For information about current and upcoming titles, please call or write, without obligation, to:

Publisher
Thorndike Press
295 Kennedy Memorial Drive
Waterville, ME 04901
Tel. (800) 223-1244

or visit our Web site at:

www.gale.com/thorndike
www.gale.com/wheeler

OR

Chivers Large Print
published by BBC Audiobooks Ltd
St James House, The Square
Lower Bristol Road
Bath BA2 3SB
England
Tel. +44(0) 800 136919
email: bbcaudiobooks@bbc.co.uk
www.bbcaudiobooks.co.uk

All our Large Print titles are designed for easy reading, and all our books are made to last.